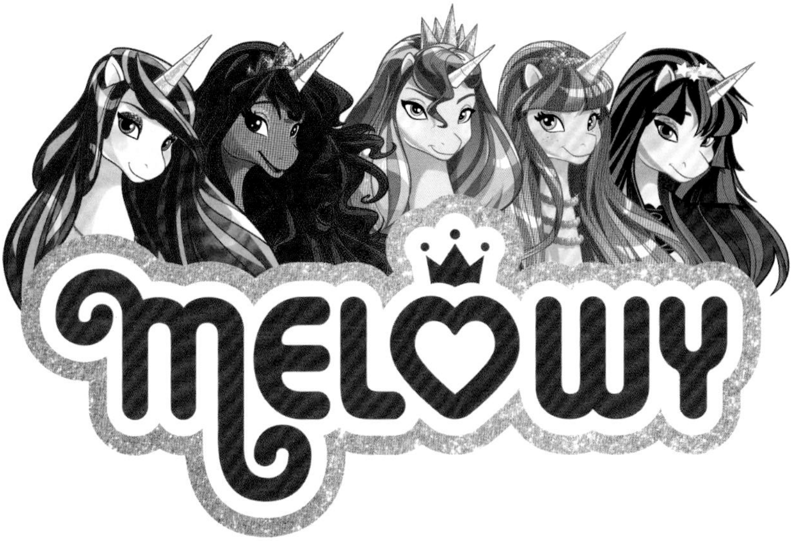

MELOWY

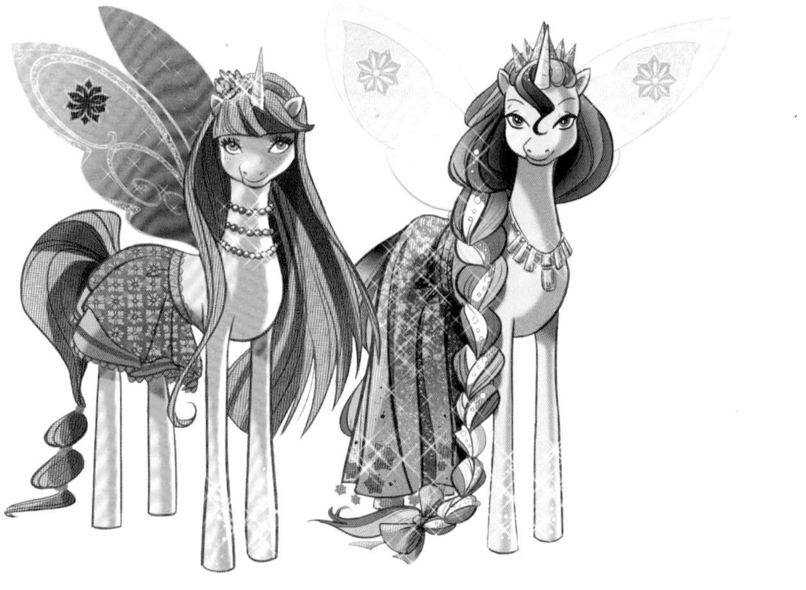

PAPERCUTZ

MORE GREAT GRAPHIC NOVEL SERIES AVAILABLE FROM PAPERCUTZ

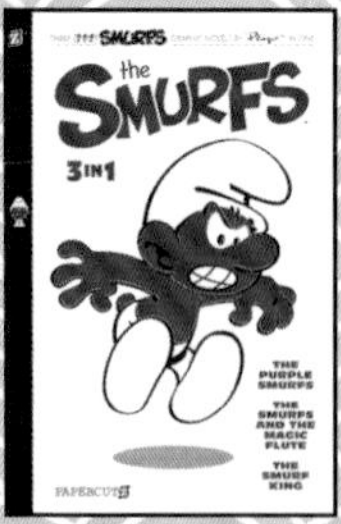
the SMURFS
3 IN 1
THE PURPLE SMURFS
THE SMURFS AND THE MAGIC FLUTE
THE SMURF KING
PAPERCUTZ
THE SMURFS 3 IN 1 #1

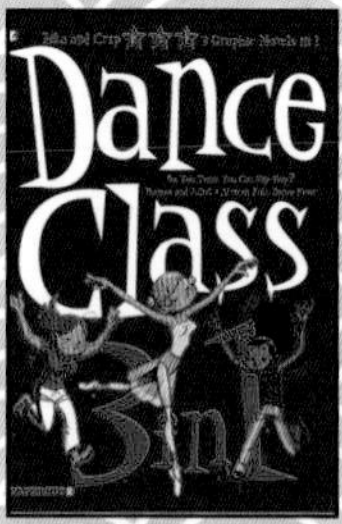
Dance Class
3 in 1
DANCE CLASS 3 IN 1 #1

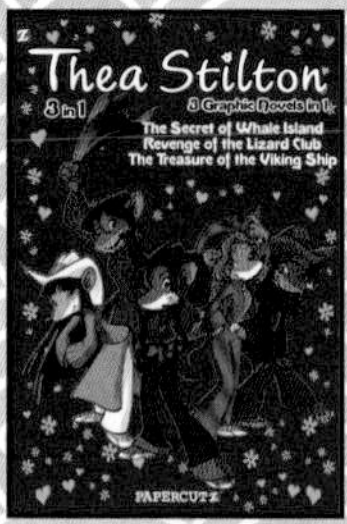
Thea Stilton
3 in 1
3 Graphic Novels in 1
The Secret of Whale Island
Revenge of the Lizard Club
The Treasure of the Viking Ship
PAPERCUTZ
THEA STILTON 3 IN 1 #1

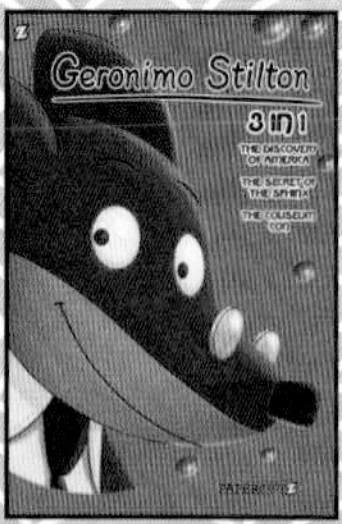
Geronimo Stilton
3 IN 1
GERONIMO STILTON 3 IN 1 #1

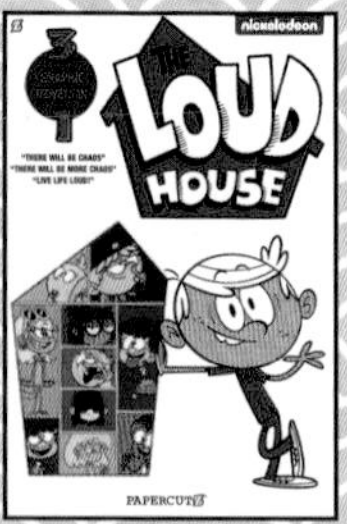
nickelodeon
THE LOUD HOUSE
PAPERCUTZ
THE LOUD HOUSE 3 IN 1 #1

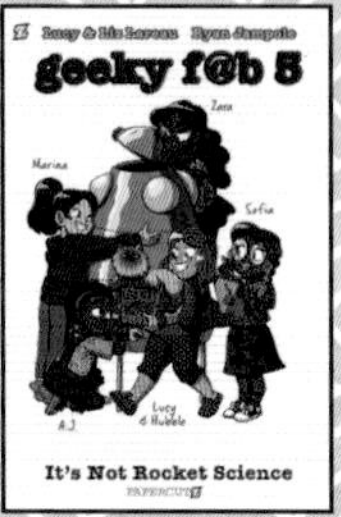
geeky f@b 5
It's Not Rocket Science
PAPERCUTZ
GEEKY F@B 5 #1

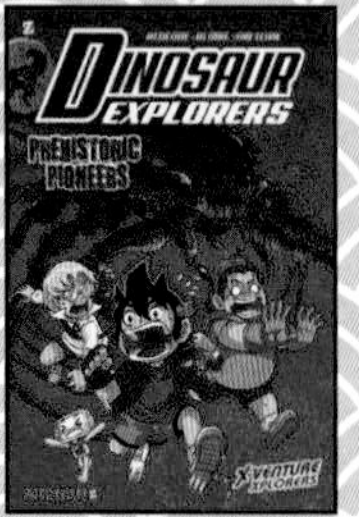
DINOSAUR EXPLORERS
PREHISTORIC PIONEERS
DINOSAUR EXPLORERS #1

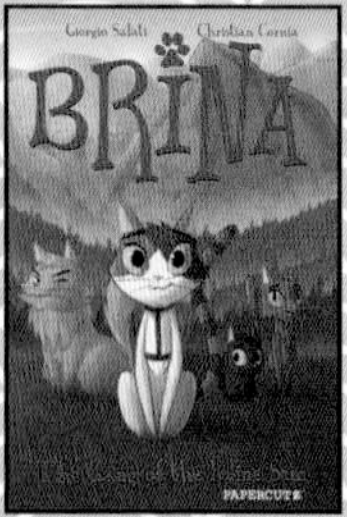
BRINA
PAPERCUTZ
BRINA THE CAT #1

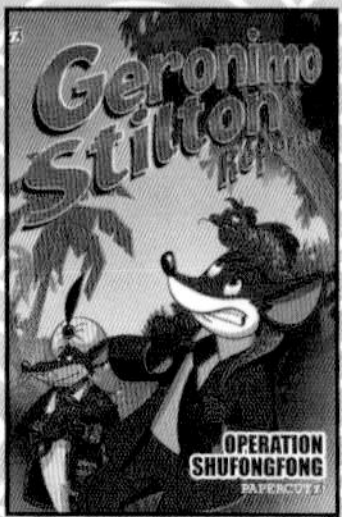
Geronimo Stilton Reporter
OPERATION SHUFONGFONG
GERONIMO STILTON REPORTER #1

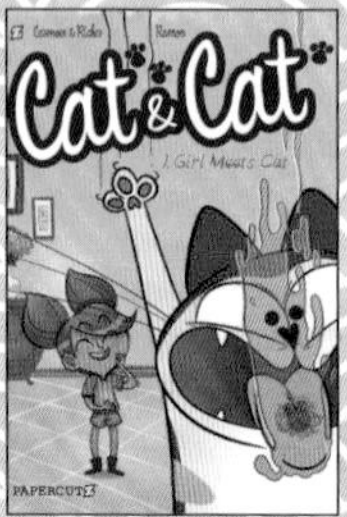
Cat & Cat
PAPERCUTZ
CAT & CAT #1

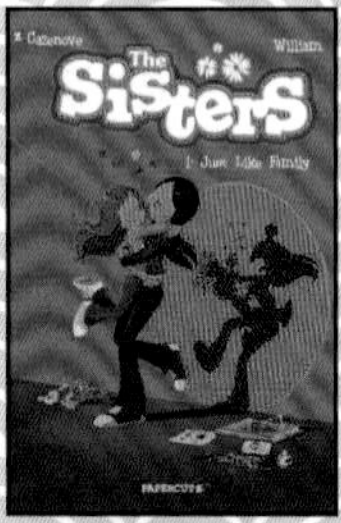
The Sisters
PAPERCUTZ
THE SISTERS #1

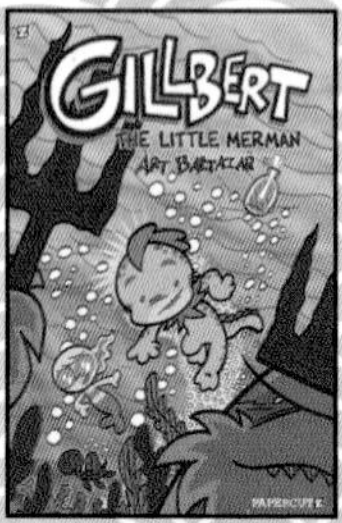
GILLBERT
THE LITTLE MERMAN
ART BALTAZAR
PAPERCUTZ
GILLBERT #1

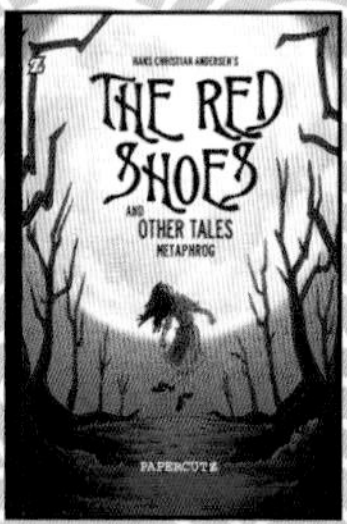
HANS CHRISTIAN ANDERSEN'S
THE RED SHOES
AND OTHER TALES
METAPHROG
PAPERCUTZ
THE RED SHOES

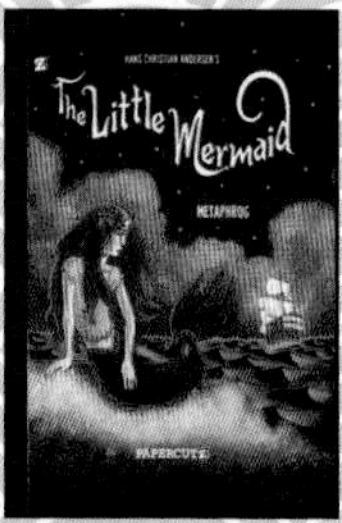
HANS CHRISTIAN ANDERSEN'S
The Little Mermaid
METAPHROG
PAPERCUTZ
THE LITTLE MERMAID

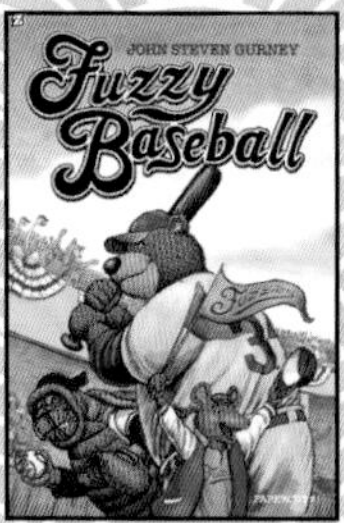
JOHN STEVEN GURNEY
Fuzzy Baseball
FUZZY BASEBALL

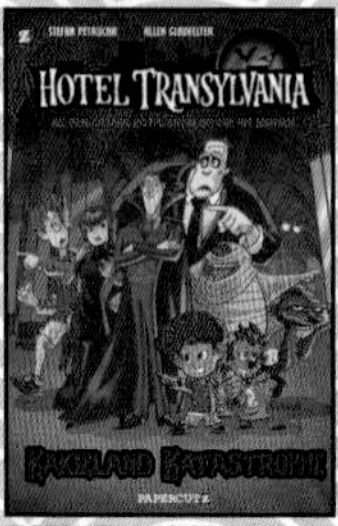
HOTEL TRANSYLVANIA
PAPERCUTZ
HOTEL TRANSYLVANIA #1

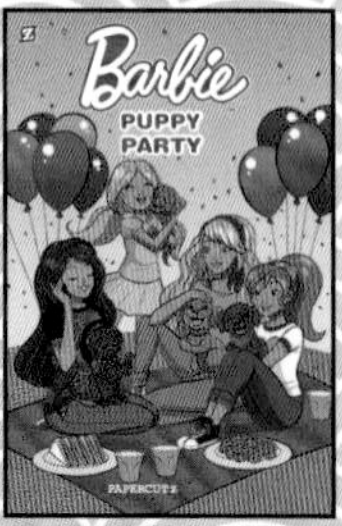
Barbie
PUPPY PARTY
PAPERCUTZ
BARBIE PUPPY PARTY #1

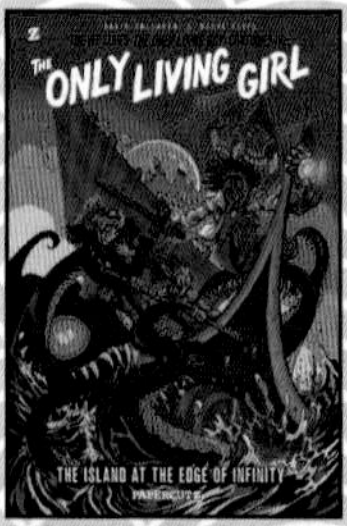
THE ONLY LIVING GIRL
THE ISLAND AT THE EDGE OF INFINITY
THE ONLY LIVING GIRL #1

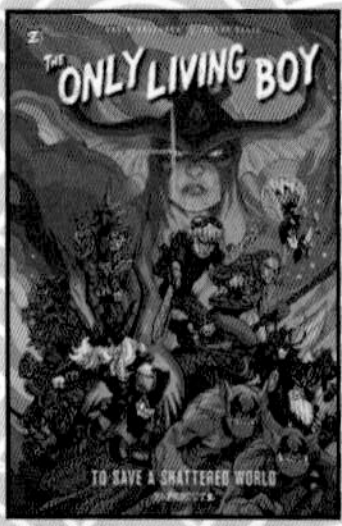
THE ONLY LIVING BOY
TO SAVE A SHATTERED WORLD
THE ONLY LIVING BOY #5

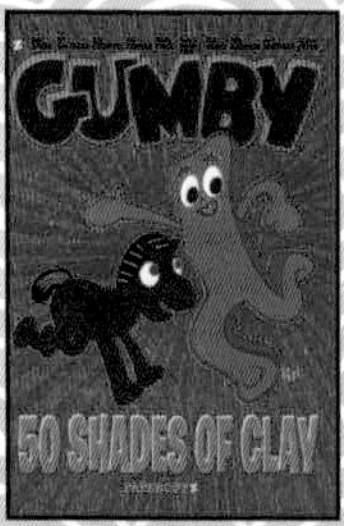
GUMBY
50 SHADES OF CLAY
PAPERCUTZ
GUMBY #1

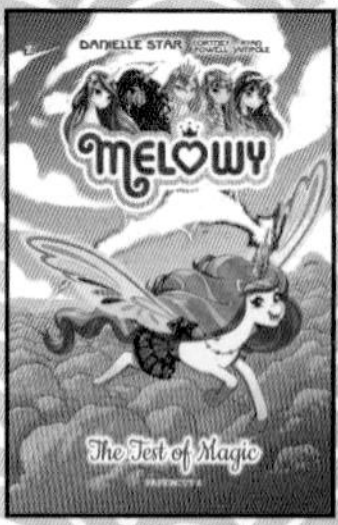
DANIELLE STAR
MELOWY
The Test of Magic
MELOWY #1

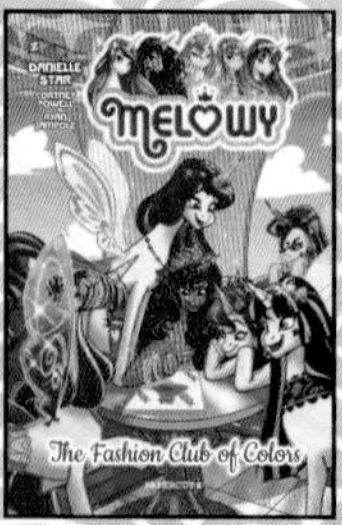
MELOWY
The Fashion Club of Colors
MELOWY #2

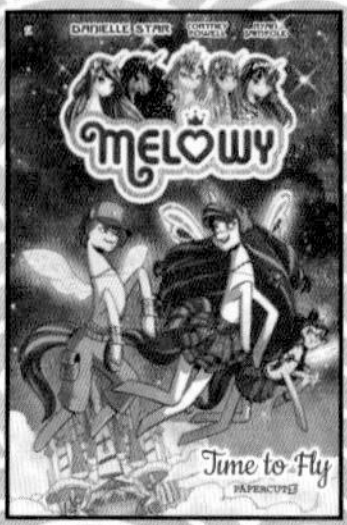
DANIELLE STAR
MELOWY
Time to Fly
PAPERCUTZ
MELOWY #3

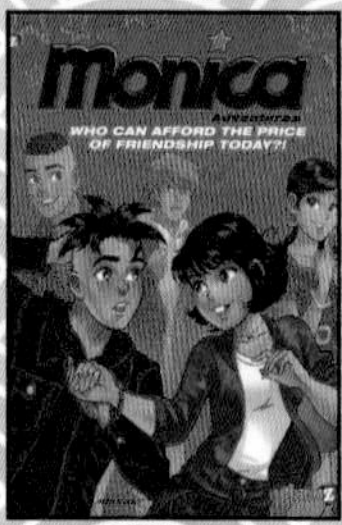
Monica
Adventures
WHO CAN AFFORD THE PRICE OF FRIENDSHIP TODAY?!
MONICA ADVENTURES #1

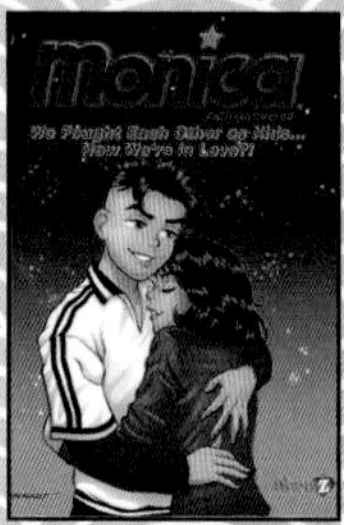
Monica
Adventures
We Fought Each Other as Kids... Now We're in Love?!
MONICA ADVENTURES #2

Go to papercutz.com for more!

THE SMURFS, DANCE CLASS, BARBIE, GERONIMO STILTON, THE LOUD HOUSE, GEEKY FAB 5, DINOSAUR EXPLORERS, BRINA THE CAT, CAT & CAT, THE SISTERS, GILLBERT, THE RED SHOES, THE LITTLE MERMAID, FUZZY BAS HOTEL TRANSYLVANIA, THE ONLY LIVING BOY, THE ONLY LIVING GIRL, and GUMBY graphic novels are also available wherever e-books are sold.

Frozen in Time

Script by **Cortney Powell**
Art by **Ryan Jampole**

PAPERCUT ™
New York

MELOWY #4
"Frozen in Time"

Copyright ©2020 by Atlantyca S.p.A., Italia.
© 2020 for this Work in English language by Papercutz.
All rights reserved.

Cover by RYAN JAMPOLE
Editorial supervision by ALESSANDRA BERELLO and LISA CAPIOTTO
(Atlantyca S.p.A.)
Script by CORTNEY POWELL
Art by RYAN JAMPOLE
Color by LAURIE E. SMITH, JAYJAY JACKSON, and LEONARDO ITO
Lettering by WILSON RAMOS JR.

Production—JAYJAY JACKSON
Editorial Intern—IZZY BOYCE-BLANCHARD
Managing Editor—JEFF WHITMAN
JIM SALICRUP
Editor-in-Chief

HC ISBN: 978-1-5458-0350-9
PB ISBN: 978-1-5458-0362-2

Printed in China
March 2020

Papercutz books may be purchased for business or promotional use.
For information on bulk purchases, please contact Macmillan
Corporate and Premium Sales Department at (800) 221-7945 x5442.

Distributed by Macmillan
First Printing

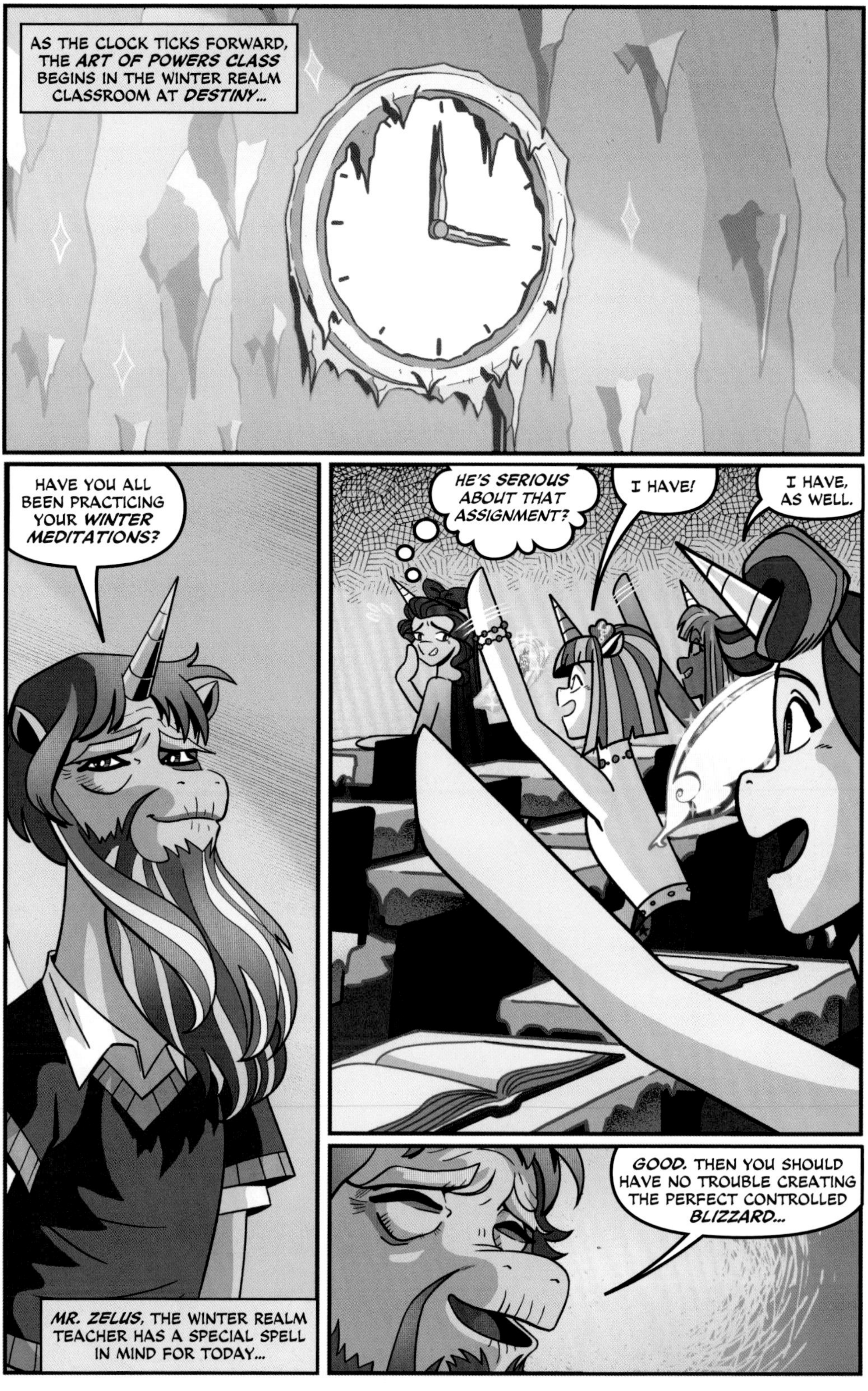
AS THE CLOCK TICKS FORWARD, THE ART OF POWERS CLASS BEGINS IN THE WINTER REALM CLASSROOM AT DESTINY...
HAVE YOU ALL BEEN PRACTICING YOUR WINTER MEDITATIONS?
MR. ZELUS, THE WINTER REALM TEACHER HAS A SPECIAL SPELL IN MIND FOR TODAY...
HE'S SERIOUS ABOUT THAT ASSIGNMENT?
I HAVE!
I HAVE, AS WELL.
GOOD. THEN YOU SHOULD HAVE NO TROUBLE CREATING THE PERFECT CONTROLLED BLIZZARD...

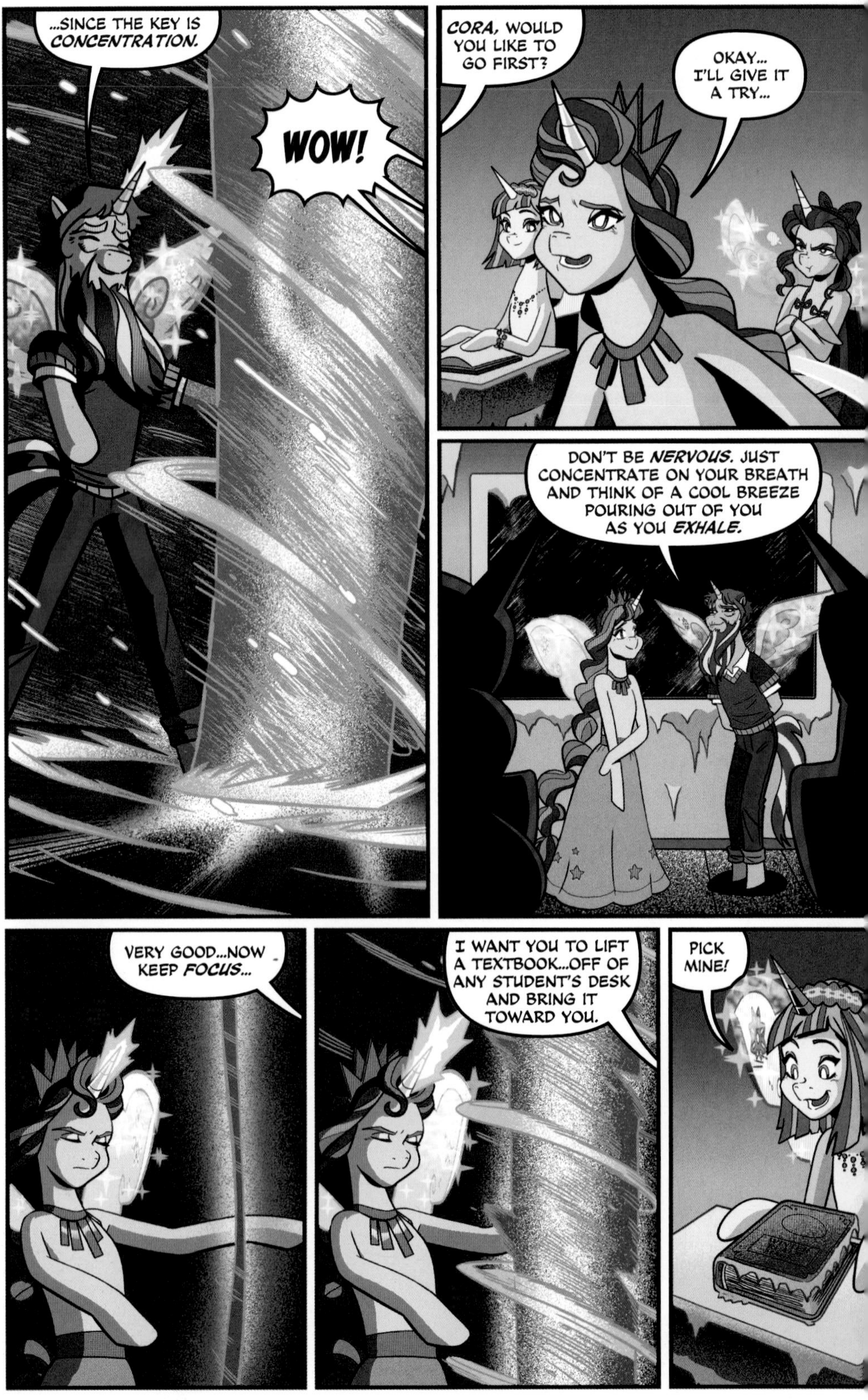

...SINCE THE KEY IS *CONCENTRATION.*
WOW!
CORA, WOULD YOU LIKE TO GO FIRST?
OKAY... I'LL GIVE IT A TRY...
DON'T BE *NERVOUS.* JUST CONCENTRATE ON YOUR BREATH AND THINK OF A COOL BREEZE POURING OUT OF YOU AS YOU *EXHALE.*
VERY GOOD...NOW KEEP *FOCUS...*
I WANT YOU TO LIFT A TEXTBOOK...OFF OF ANY STUDENT'S DESK AND BRING IT TOWARD YOU.
PICK MINE!

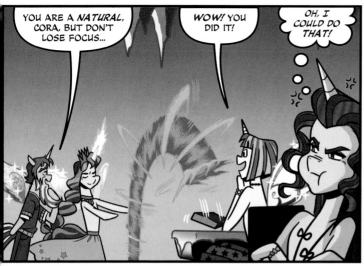

YOU ARE A *NATURAL*, CORA, BUT DON'T LOSE FOCUS...

WOW! YOU DID IT!

OH, I COULD DO *THAT!*

MR. ZELUS, SORRY TO INTERRUPT BUT I NEED TO SPEAK WITH YOU *IMMEDIATELY.*

I'LL BE RIGHT THERE, *PRINCIPAL GIA.* I'LL ONLY BE A MOMENT, STUDENTS.

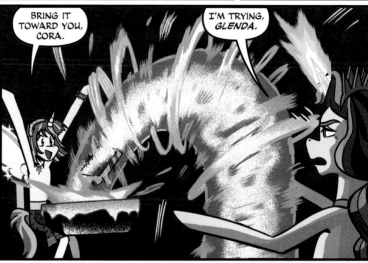

BRING IT TOWARD YOU, CORA.

I'M TRYING, *GLENDA.*

DO YOU NEED HELP?

COME ON, LET *ME* TRY!

IT IS A LOT HARDER THAN IT LOOKS, *ERIS*, YOU REALLY HAVE TO CONCENTRATE.

I KNEW I COULD DO IT.

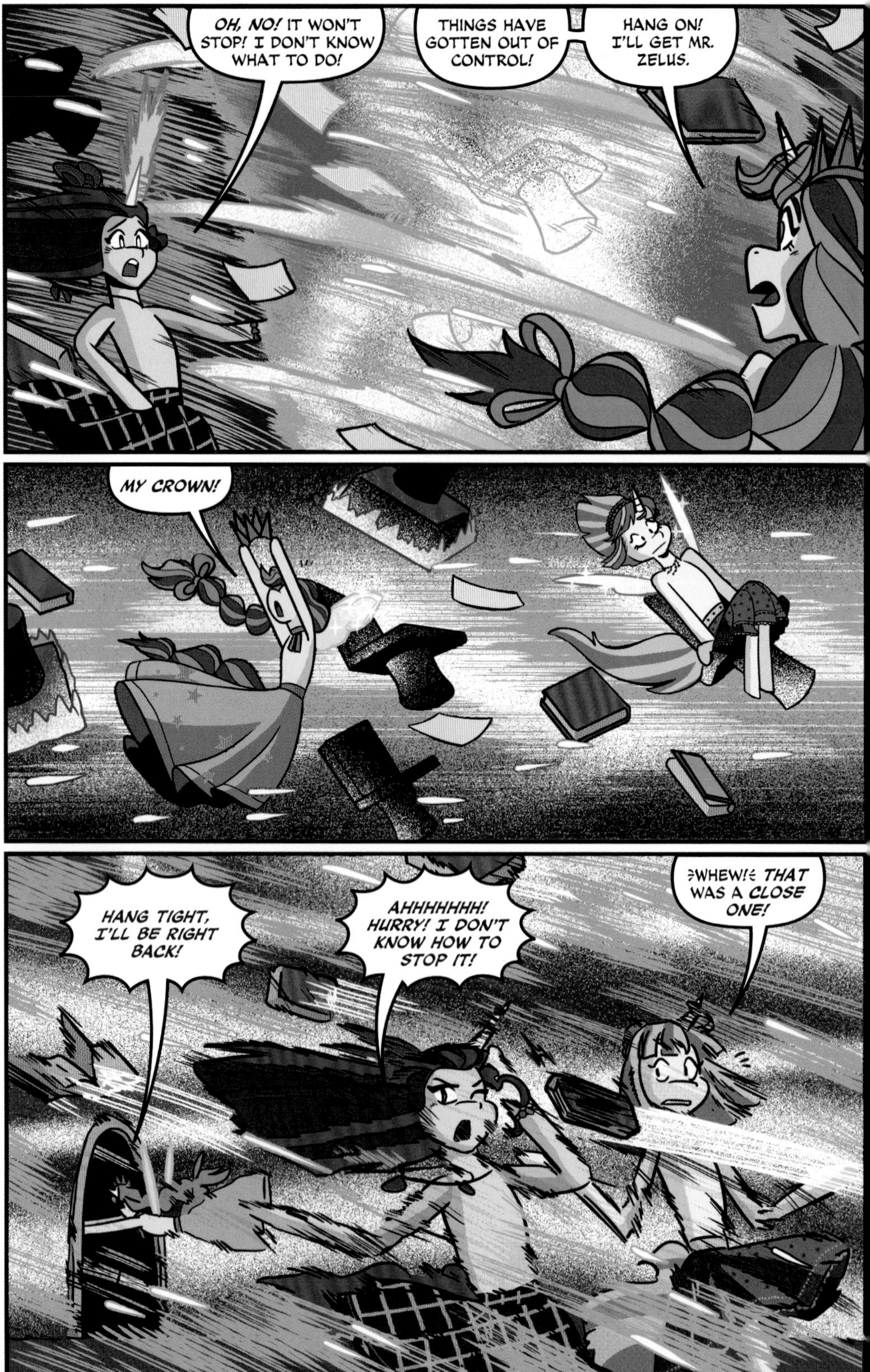
OH, NO! IT WON'T STOP! I DON'T KNOW WHAT TO DO!
THINGS HAVE GOTTEN OUT OF CONTROL!
HANG ON! I'LL GET MR. ZELUS.
MY CROWN!
HANG TIGHT, I'LL BE RIGHT BACK!
AHHHHHHH! HURRY! I DON'T KNOW HOW TO STOP IT!
WHEW! THAT WAS A CLOSE ONE!

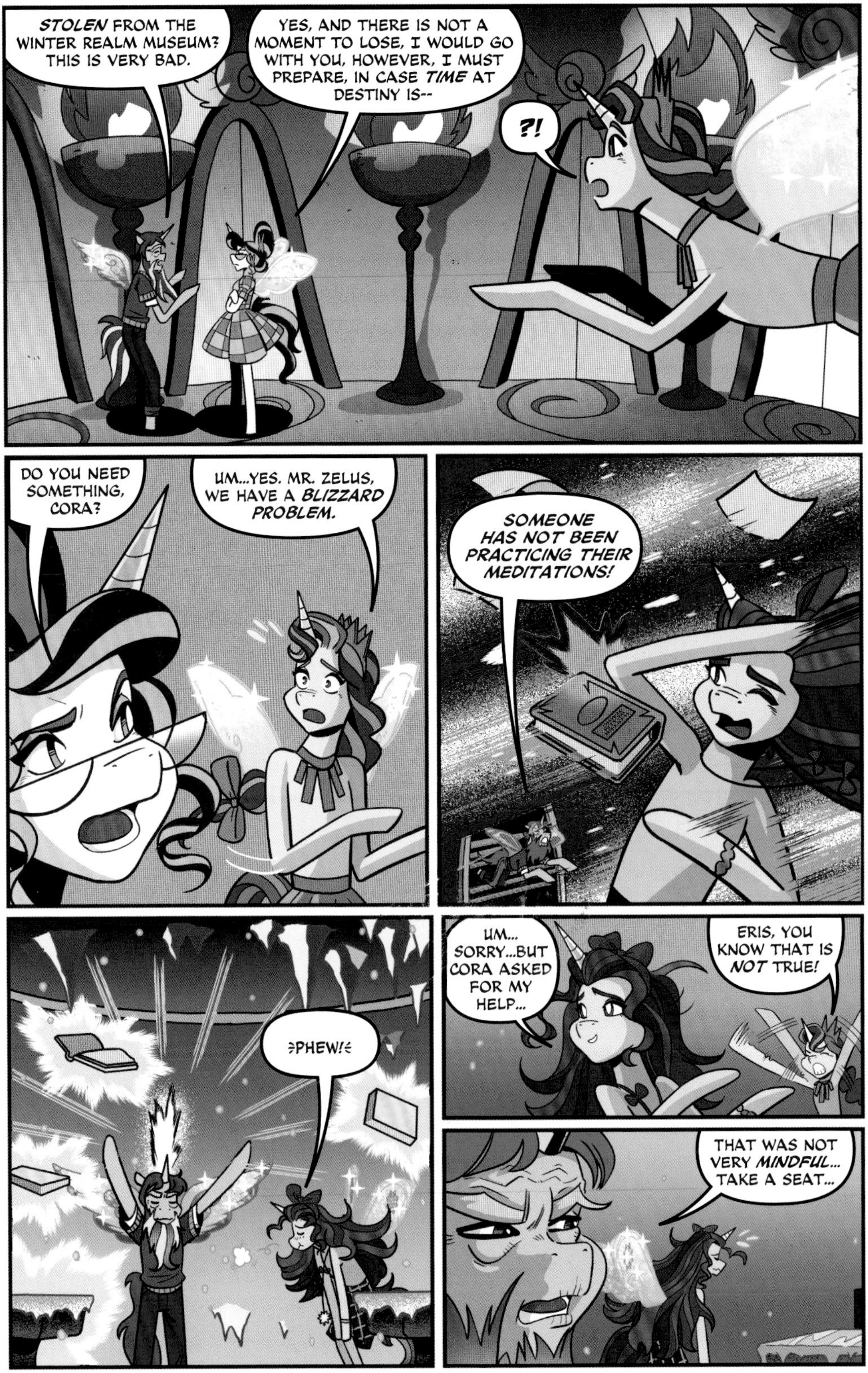
STOLEN FROM THE WINTER REALM MUSEUM? THIS IS VERY BAD.
YES, AND THERE IS NOT A MOMENT TO LOSE, I WOULD GO WITH YOU, HOWEVER, I MUST PREPARE, IN CASE TIME AT DESTINY IS--
?!
DO YOU NEED SOMETHING, CORA?
UM...YES. MR. ZELUS, WE HAVE A BLIZZARD PROBLEM.
SOMEONE HAS NOT BEEN PRACTICING THEIR MEDITATIONS!
PHEW!
UM... SORRY...BUT CORA ASKED FOR MY HELP...
ERIS, YOU KNOW THAT IS NOT TRUE!
THAT WAS NOT VERY MINDFUL... TAKE A SEAT...

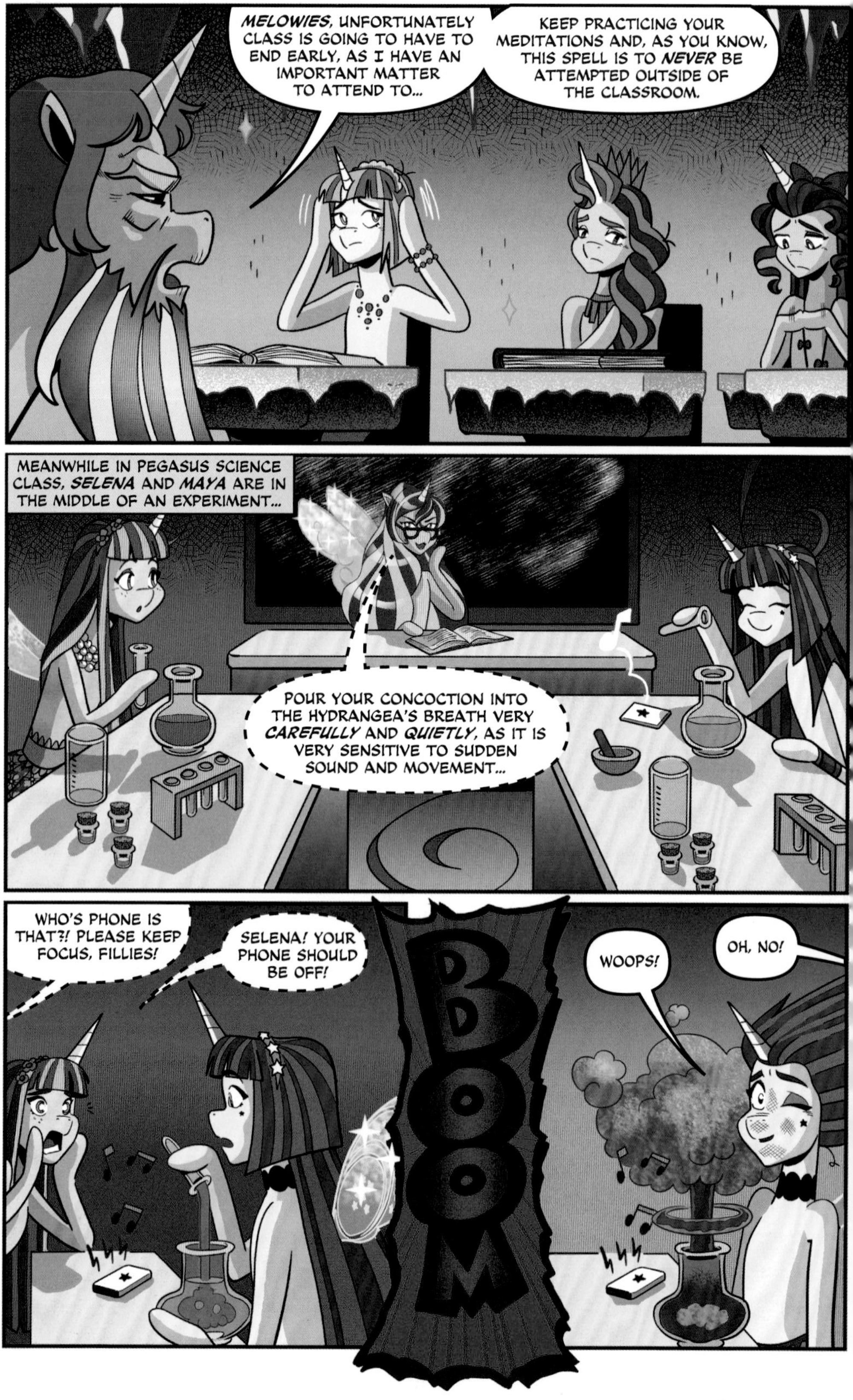

MELOWIES, UNFORTUNATELY CLASS IS GOING TO HAVE TO END EARLY, AS I HAVE AN IMPORTANT MATTER TO ATTEND TO...
KEEP PRACTICING YOUR MEDITATIONS AND, AS YOU KNOW, THIS SPELL IS TO NEVER BE ATTEMPTED OUTSIDE OF THE CLASSROOM.
MEANWHILE IN PEGASUS SCIENCE CLASS, SELENA AND MAYA ARE IN THE MIDDLE OF AN EXPERIMENT...
POUR YOUR CONCOCTION INTO THE HYDRANGEA'S BREATH VERY CAREFULLY AND QUIETLY, AS IT IS VERY SENSITIVE TO SUDDEN SOUND AND MOVEMENT...
WHO'S PHONE IS THAT?! PLEASE KEEP FOCUS, FILLIES!
SELENA! YOUR PHONE SHOULD BE OFF!
BOOM
WOOPS!
OH, NO!

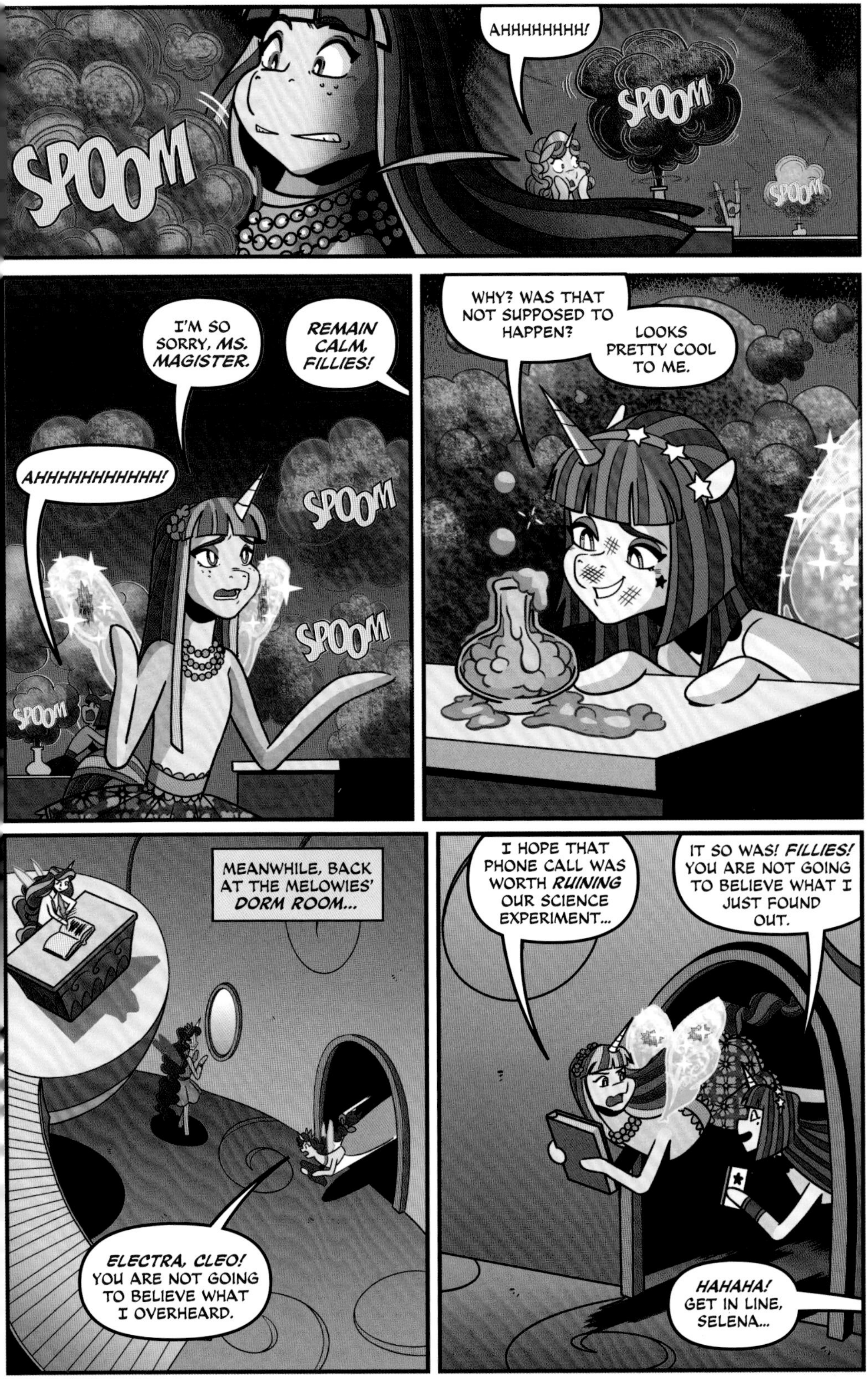
SPOOM
AHHHHHHHH!
SPOOM
SPOOM
I'M SO SORRY, MS. MAGISTER.
REMAIN CALM, FILLIES!
AHHHHHHHHHHH!
SPOOM
SPOOM
SPOOM
WHY? WAS THAT NOT SUPPOSED TO HAPPEN?
LOOKS PRETTY COOL TO ME.
MEANWHILE, BACK AT THE MELOWIES' DORM ROOM...
ELECTRA, CLEO! YOU ARE NOT GOING TO BELIEVE WHAT I OVERHEARD.
I HOPE THAT PHONE CALL WAS WORTH RUINING OUR SCIENCE EXPERIMENT...
IT SO WAS! FILLIES! YOU ARE NOT GOING TO BELIEVE WHAT I JUST FOUND OUT.
HAHAHA! GET IN LINE, SELENA...

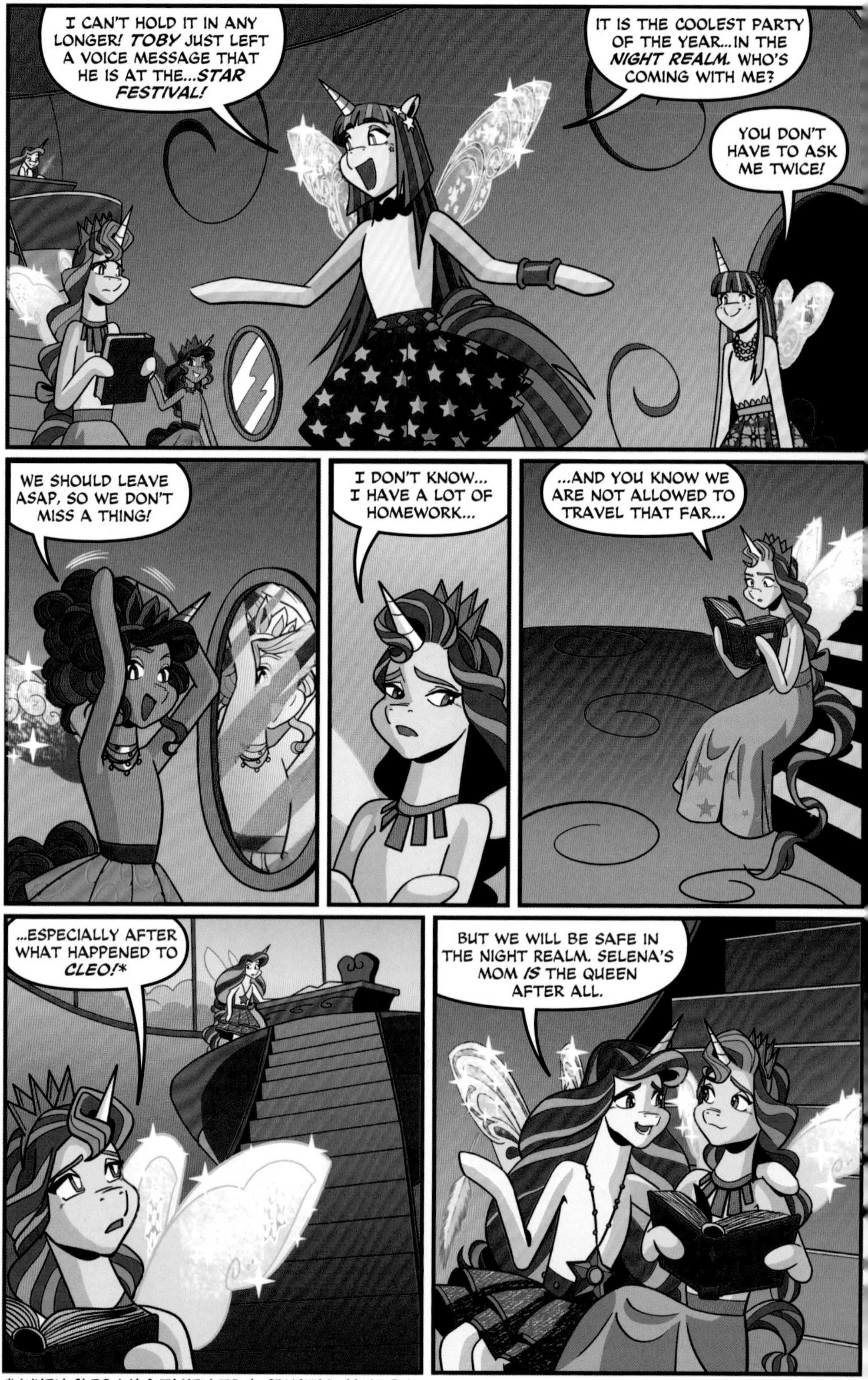
I CAN'T HOLD IT IN ANY LONGER! TOBY JUST LEFT A VOICE MESSAGE THAT HE IS AT THE...STAR FESTIVAL!
IT IS THE COOLEST PARTY OF THE YEAR...IN THE NIGHT REALM. WHO'S COMING WITH ME?
YOU DON'T HAVE TO ASK ME TWICE!
WE SHOULD LEAVE ASAP, SO WE DON'T MISS A THING!
I DON'T KNOW... I HAVE A LOT OF HOMEWORK...
...AND YOU KNOW WE ARE NOT ALLOWED TO TRAVEL THAT FAR...
...ESPECIALLY AFTER WHAT HAPPENED TO CLEO!*
BUT WE WILL BE SAFE IN THE NIGHT REALM. SELENA'S MOM IS THE QUEEN AFTER ALL.

* WHEN CLEO WAS TAKEN TO A CRYSTAL CAVE BY AN EVIL PEGASUS, SEE *MELOWY* #3.

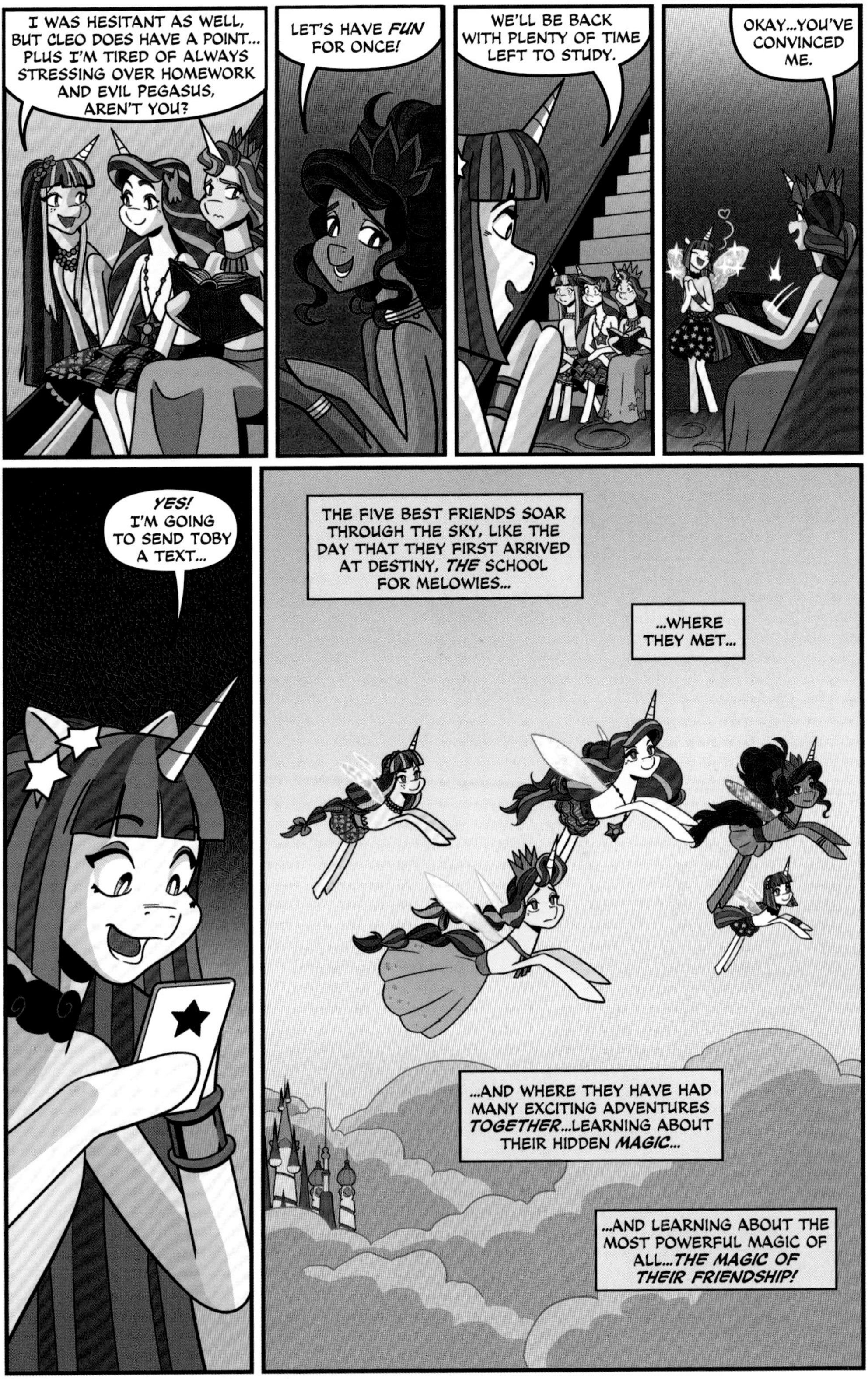
I WAS HESITANT AS WELL, BUT CLEO DOES HAVE A POINT... PLUS I'M TIRED OF ALWAYS STRESSING OVER HOMEWORK AND EVIL PEGASUS, AREN'T YOU?
LET'S HAVE *FUN* FOR ONCE!
WE'LL BE BACK WITH PLENTY OF TIME LEFT TO STUDY.
OKAY...YOU'VE CONVINCED ME.
YES! I'M GOING TO SEND TOBY A TEXT...
THE FIVE BEST FRIENDS SOAR THROUGH THE SKY, LIKE THE DAY THAT THEY FIRST ARRIVED AT DESTINY, *THE* SCHOOL FOR MELOWIES...
...WHERE THEY MET...
...AND WHERE THEY HAVE HAD MANY EXCITING ADVENTURES *TOGETHER*...LEARNING ABOUT THEIR HIDDEN *MAGIC*...
...AND LEARNING ABOUT THE MOST POWERFUL MAGIC OF ALL...*THE MAGIC OF THEIR FRIENDSHIP!*

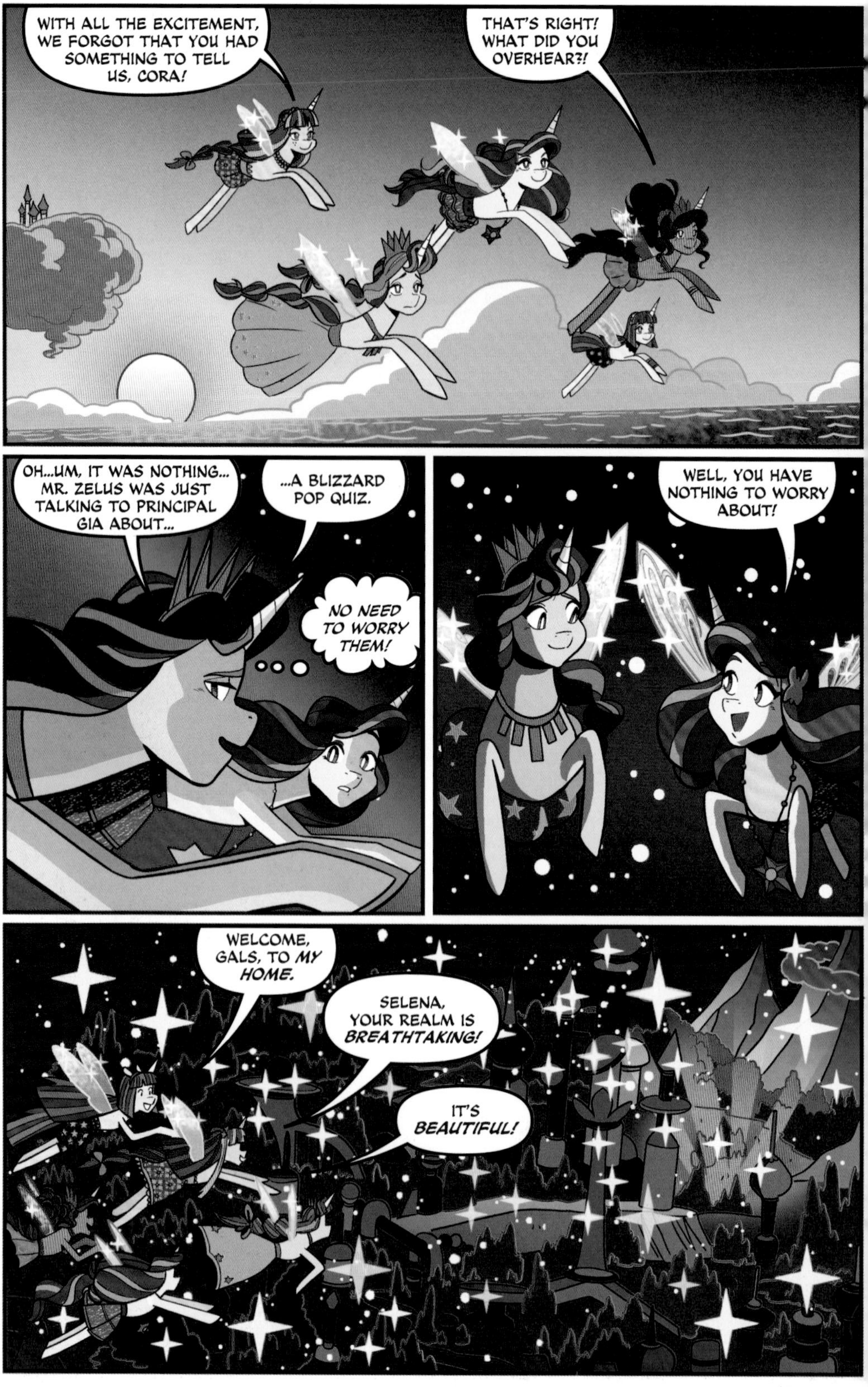
WITH ALL THE EXCITEMENT, WE FORGOT THAT YOU HAD SOMETHING TO TELL US, CORA!
THAT'S RIGHT! WHAT DID YOU OVERHEAR?!
OH...UM, IT WAS NOTHING... MR. ZELUS WAS JUST TALKING TO PRINCIPAL GIA ABOUT...
...A BLIZZARD POP QUIZ.
NO NEED TO WORRY THEM!
WELL, YOU HAVE NOTHING TO WORRY ABOUT!
WELCOME, GALS, TO *MY HOME.*
SELENA, YOUR REALM IS *BREATHTAKING!*
IT'S *BEAUTIFUL!*

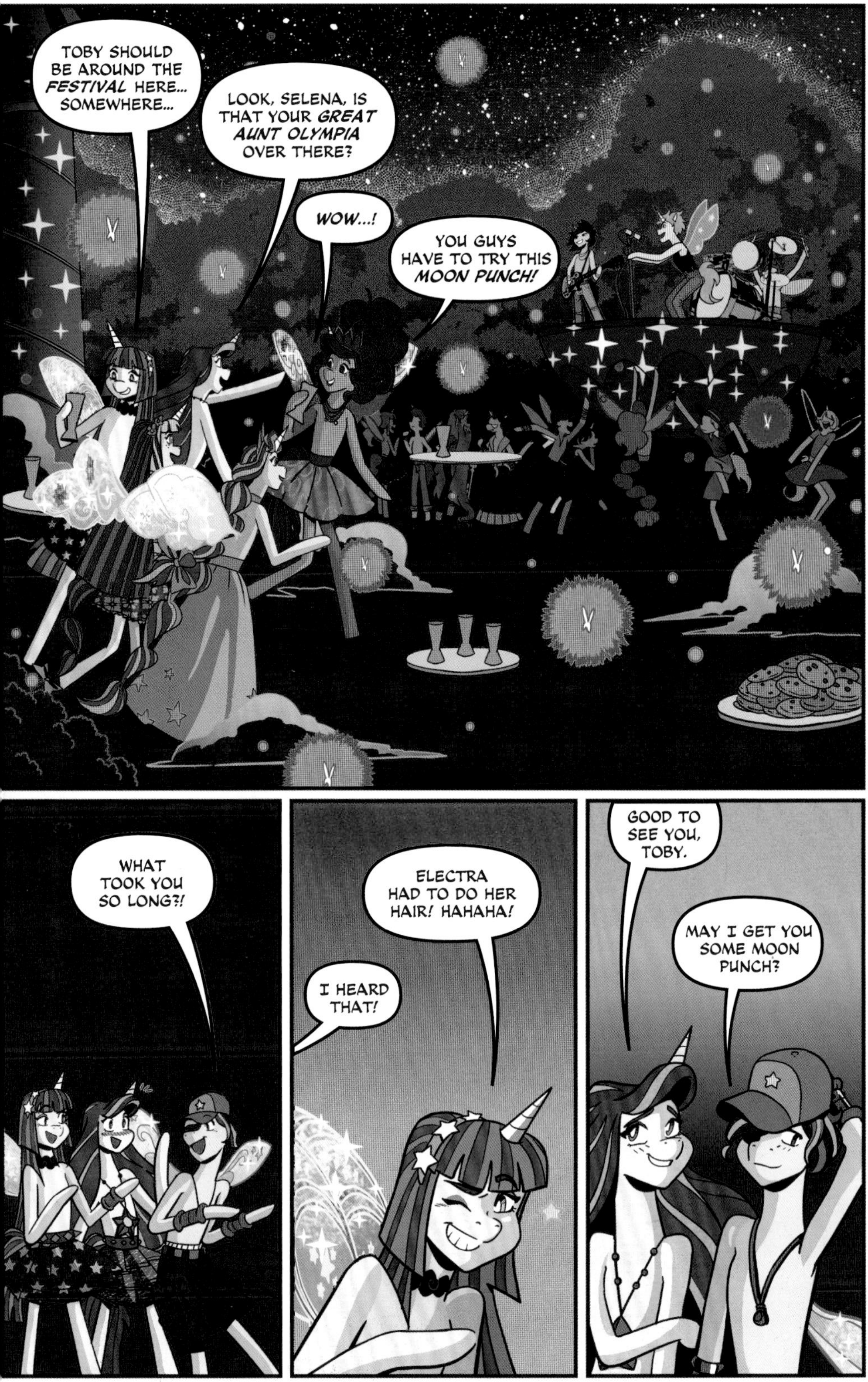
TOBY SHOULD BE AROUND THE *FESTIVAL* HERE... SOMEWHERE...
LOOK, SELENA, IS THAT YOUR *GREAT AUNT OLYMPIA* OVER THERE?
WOW...!
YOU GUYS HAVE TO TRY THIS *MOON PUNCH!*
WHAT TOOK YOU SO LONG?!
ELECTRA HAD TO DO HER HAIR! HAHAHA!
I HEARD THAT!
GOOD TO SEE YOU, TOBY.
MAY I GET YOU SOME MOON PUNCH?

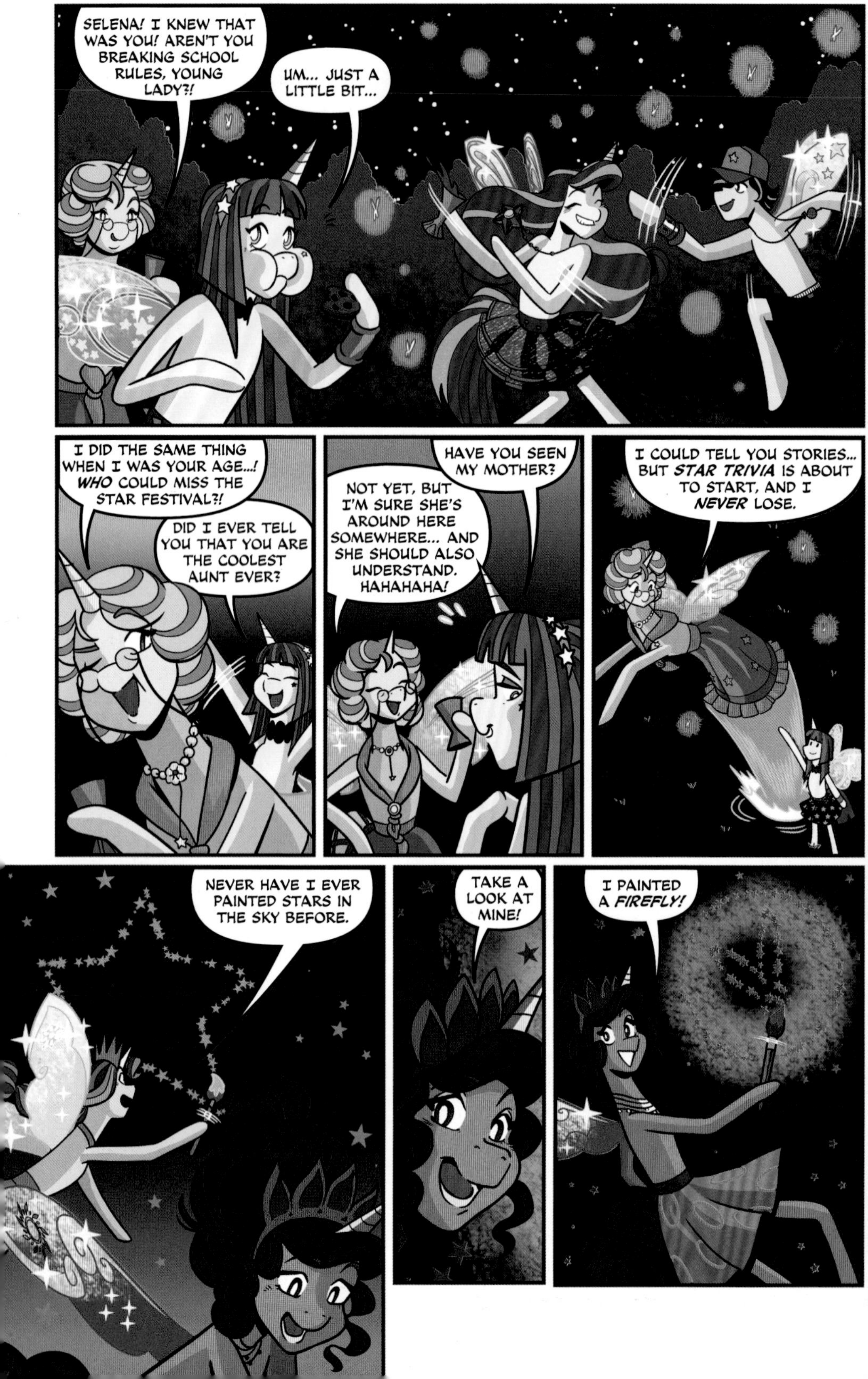
SELENA! I KNEW THAT WAS YOU! AREN'T YOU BREAKING SCHOOL RULES, YOUNG LADY?!
UM... JUST A LITTLE BIT...
I DID THE SAME THING WHEN I WAS YOUR AGE...! WHO COULD MISS THE STAR FESTIVAL?!
DID I EVER TELL YOU THAT YOU ARE THE COOLEST AUNT EVER?
HAVE YOU SEEN MY MOTHER?
NOT YET, BUT I'M SURE SHE'S AROUND HERE SOMEWHERE... AND SHE SHOULD ALSO UNDERSTAND. HAHAHAHA!
I COULD TELL YOU STORIES... BUT STAR TRIVIA IS ABOUT TO START, AND I NEVER LOSE.
NEVER HAVE I EVER PAINTED STARS IN THE SKY BEFORE.
TAKE A LOOK AT MINE!
I PAINTED A FIREFLY!

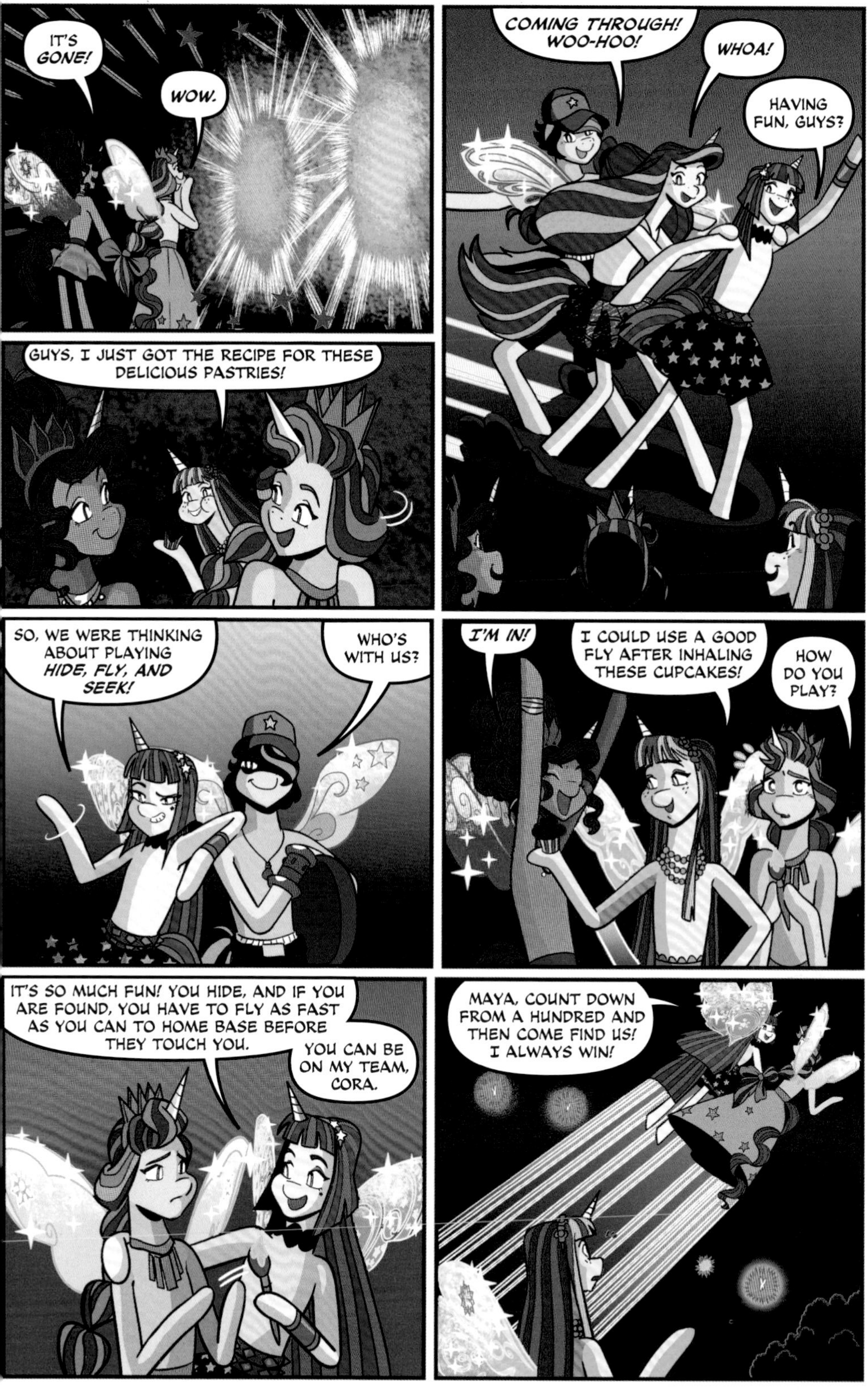
IT'S GONE!
WOW.
COMING THROUGH! WOO-HOO!
WHOA!
HAVING FUN, GUYS?
GUYS, I JUST GOT THE RECIPE FOR THESE DELICIOUS PASTRIES!
SO, WE WERE THINKING ABOUT PLAYING *HIDE, FLY, AND SEEK!*
WHO'S WITH US?
I'M IN!
I COULD USE A GOOD FLY AFTER INHALING THESE CUPCAKES!
HOW DO YOU PLAY?
IT'S SO MUCH FUN! YOU HIDE, AND IF YOU ARE FOUND, YOU HAVE TO FLY AS FAST AS YOU CAN TO HOME BASE BEFORE THEY TOUCH YOU.
YOU CAN BE ON MY TEAM, CORA.
MAYA, COUNT DOWN FROM A HUNDRED AND THEN COME FIND US! I ALWAYS WIN!

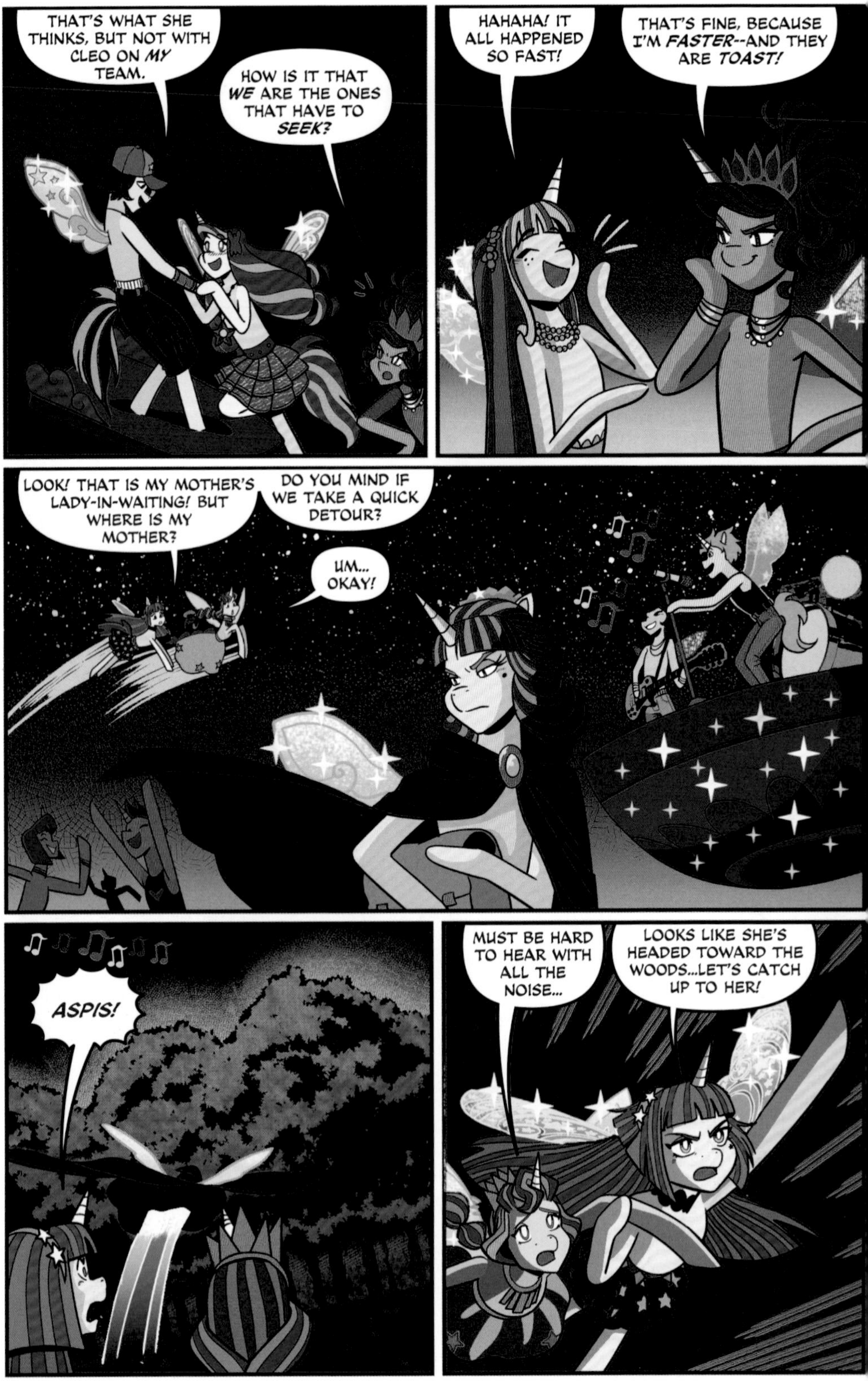
THAT'S WHAT SHE THINKS, BUT NOT WITH CLEO ON MY TEAM.
HOW IS IT THAT WE ARE THE ONES THAT HAVE TO SEEK?
HAHAHA! IT ALL HAPPENED SO FAST!
THAT'S FINE, BECAUSE I'M FASTER--AND THEY ARE TOAST!
LOOK! THAT IS MY MOTHER'S LADY-IN-WAITING! BUT WHERE IS MY MOTHER?
DO YOU MIND IF WE TAKE A QUICK DETOUR?
UM... OKAY!
ASPIS!
MUST BE HARD TO HEAR WITH ALL THE NOISE...
LOOKS LIKE SHE'S HEADED TOWARD THE WOODS...LET'S CATCH UP TO HER!

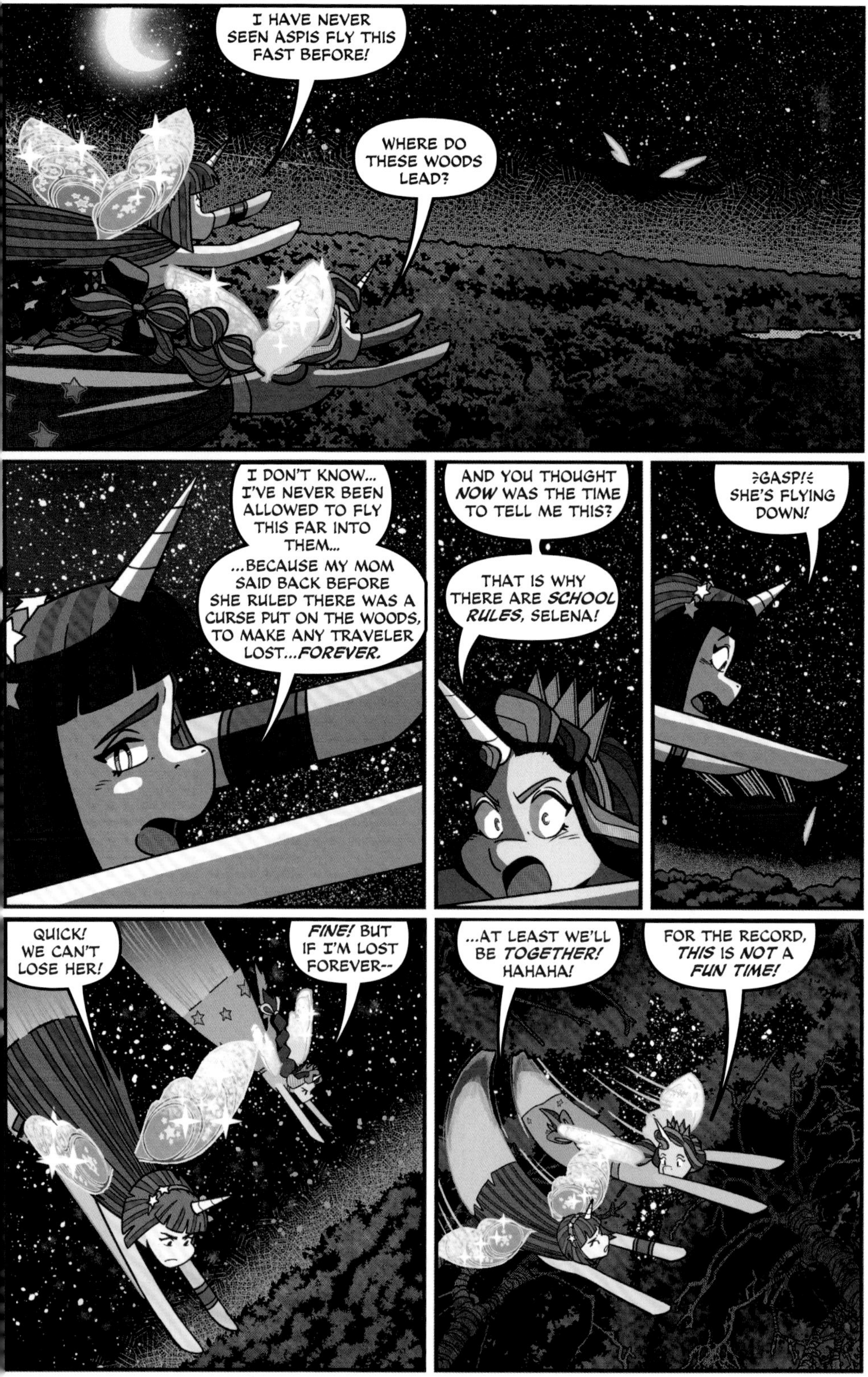
I HAVE NEVER SEEN ASPIS FLY THIS FAST BEFORE!
WHERE DO THESE WOODS LEAD?
I DON'T KNOW... I'VE NEVER BEEN ALLOWED TO FLY THIS FAR INTO THEM...
...BECAUSE MY MOM SAID BACK BEFORE SHE RULED THERE WAS A CURSE PUT ON THE WOODS, TO MAKE ANY TRAVELER LOST...FOREVER.
AND YOU THOUGHT NOW WAS THE TIME TO TELL ME THIS?
THAT IS WHY THERE ARE SCHOOL RULES, SELENA!
GASP! SHE'S FLYING DOWN!
QUICK! WE CAN'T LOSE HER!
FINE! BUT IF I'M LOST FOREVER--
...AT LEAST WE'LL BE TOGETHER! HAHAHA!
FOR THE RECORD, THIS IS NOT A FUN TIME!

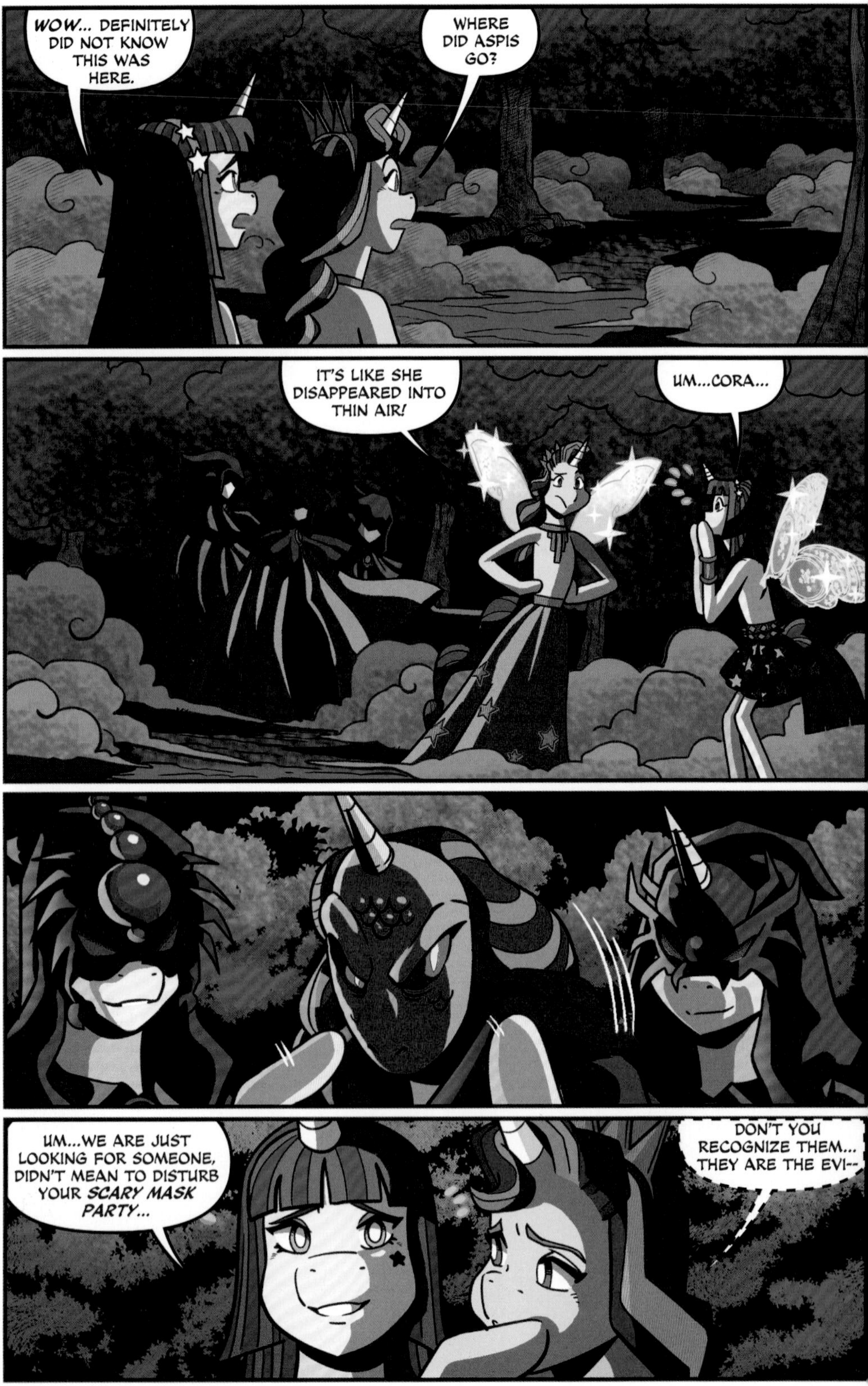
WOW... DEFINITELY DID NOT KNOW THIS WAS HERE.
WHERE DID ASPIS GO?
IT'S LIKE SHE DISAPPEARED INTO THIN AIR!
UM...CORA...
UM...WE ARE JUST LOOKING FOR SOMEONE, DIDN'T MEAN TO DISTURB YOUR SCARY MASK PARTY...
DON'T YOU RECOGNIZE THEM... THEY ARE THE EVI--

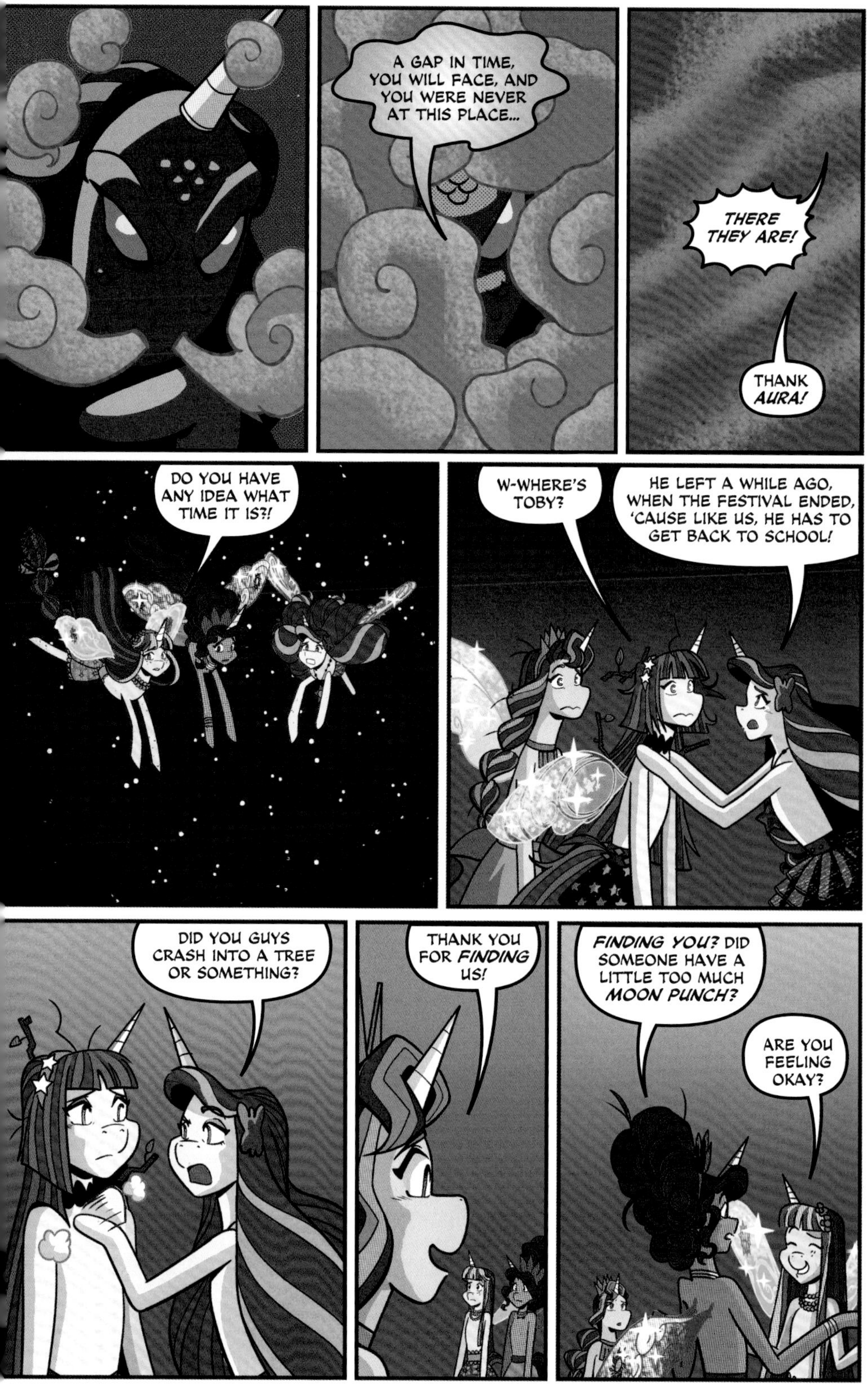

A GAP IN TIME, YOU WILL FACE, AND YOU WERE NEVER AT THIS PLACE...
THERE THEY ARE!
THANK AURA!
DO YOU HAVE ANY IDEA WHAT TIME IT IS?!
W-WHERE'S TOBY?
HE LEFT A WHILE AGO, WHEN THE FESTIVAL ENDED, 'CAUSE LIKE US, HE HAS TO GET BACK TO SCHOOL!
DID YOU GUYS CRASH INTO A TREE OR SOMETHING?
THANK YOU FOR FINDING US!
FINDING YOU? DID SOMEONE HAVE A LITTLE TOO MUCH MOON PUNCH?
ARE YOU FEELING OKAY?

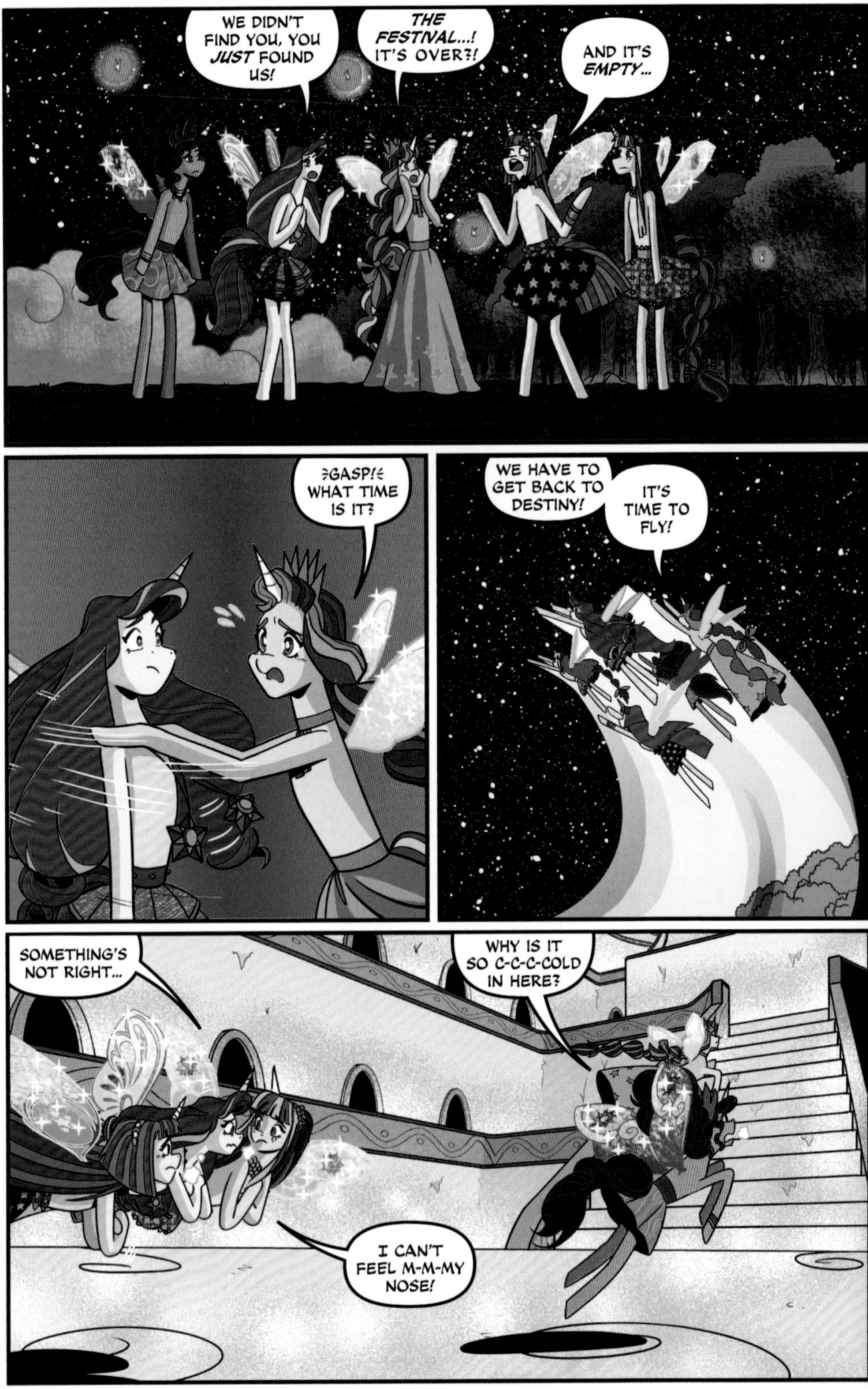
WE DIDN'T FIND YOU, YOU JUST FOUND US!
THE FESTIVAL...! IT'S OVER?!
AND IT'S EMPTY...
GASP! WHAT TIME IS IT?
WE HAVE TO GET BACK TO DESTINY!
IT'S TIME TO FLY!
SOMETHING'S NOT RIGHT...
WHY IS IT SO C-C-C-COLD IN HERE?
I CAN'T FEEL M-M-MY NOSE!

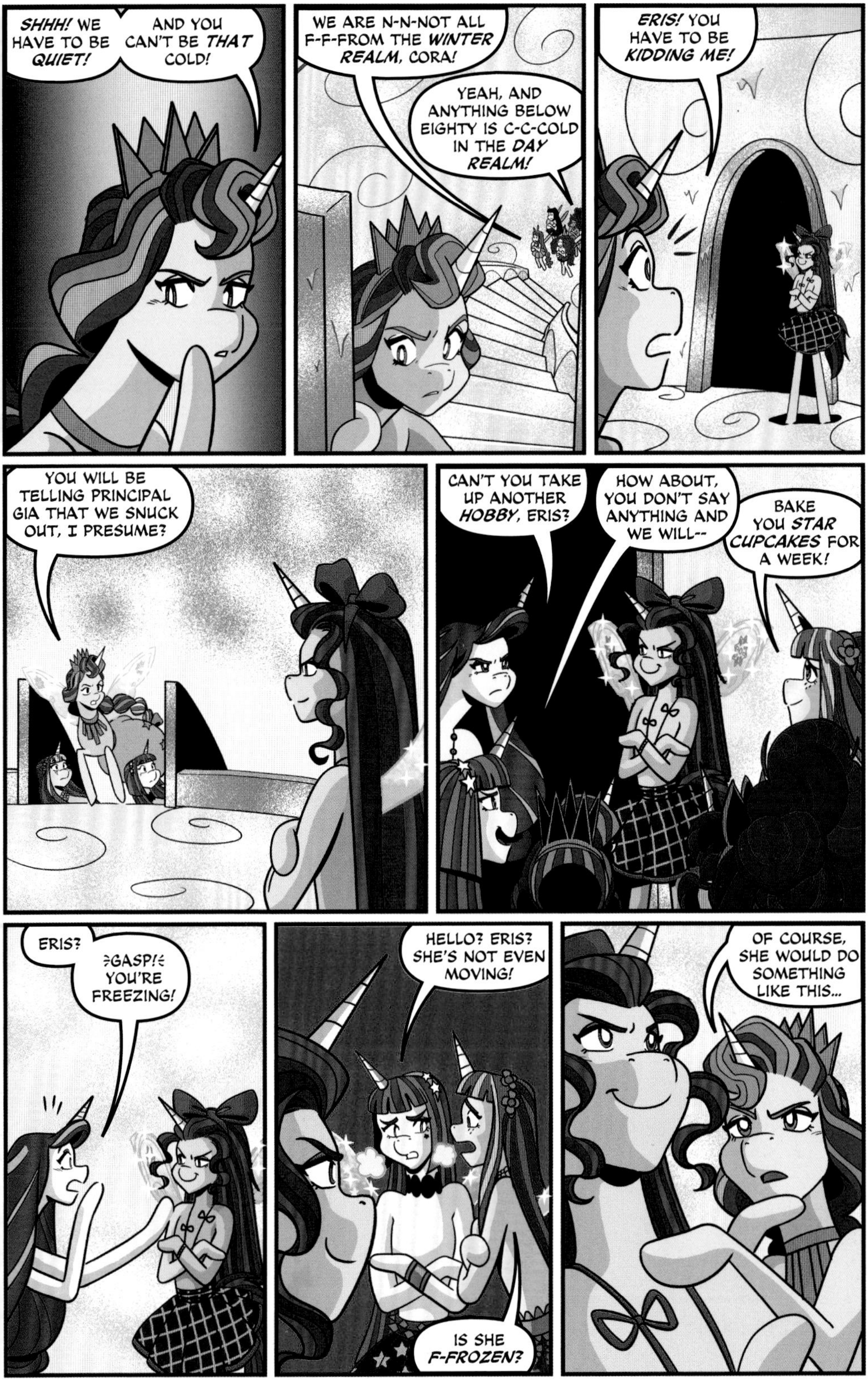
SHHH! WE HAVE TO BE QUIET!
AND YOU CAN'T BE THAT COLD!
WE ARE N-N-NOT ALL F-F-FROM THE WINTER REALM, CORA!
YEAH, AND ANYTHING BELOW EIGHTY IS C-C-COLD IN THE DAY REALM!
ERIS! YOU HAVE TO BE KIDDING ME!
YOU WILL BE TELLING PRINCIPAL GIA THAT WE SNUCK OUT, I PRESUME?
CAN'T YOU TAKE UP ANOTHER HOBBY, ERIS?
HOW ABOUT, YOU DON'T SAY ANYTHING AND WE WILL--
BAKE YOU STAR CUPCAKES FOR A WEEK!
ERIS?
GASP! YOU'RE FREEZING!
HELLO? ERIS? SHE'S NOT EVEN MOVING!
IS SHE F-FROZEN?
OF COURSE, SHE WOULD DO SOMETHING LIKE THIS...

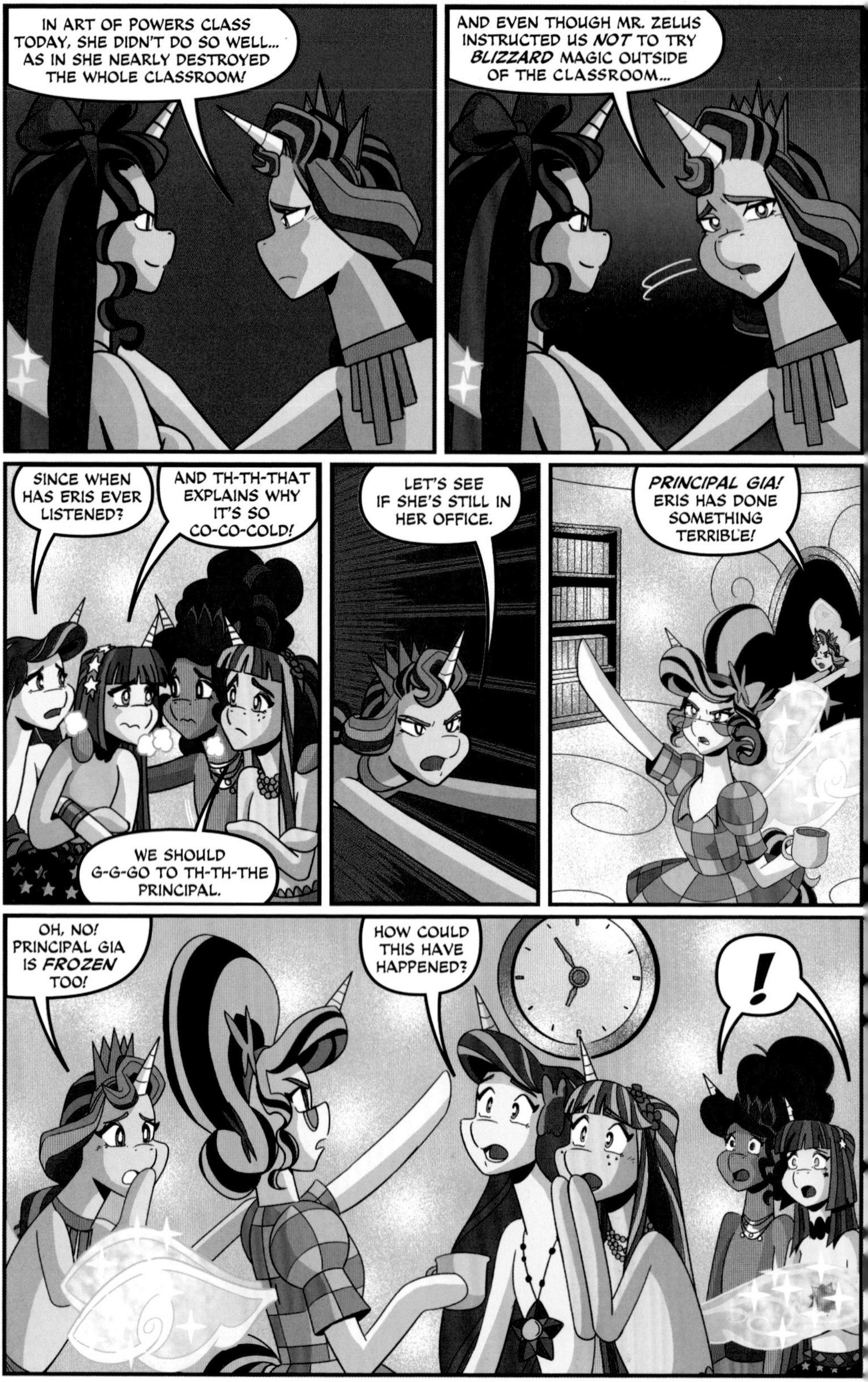
IN ART OF POWERS CLASS TODAY, SHE DIDN'T DO SO WELL... AS IN SHE NEARLY DESTROYED THE WHOLE CLASSROOM!
AND EVEN THOUGH MR. ZELUS INSTRUCTED US *NOT* TO TRY *BLIZZARD* MAGIC OUTSIDE OF THE CLASSROOM...
SINCE WHEN HAS ERIS EVER LISTENED?
AND TH-TH-THAT EXPLAINS WHY IT'S SO CO-CO-COLD!
WE SHOULD G-G-GO TO TH-TH-THE PRINCIPAL.
LET'S SEE IF SHE'S STILL IN HER OFFICE.
PRINCIPAL GIA! ERIS HAS DONE SOMETHING TERRIBLE!
OH, NO! PRINCIPAL GIA IS *FROZEN* TOO!
HOW COULD THIS HAVE HAPPENED?
!

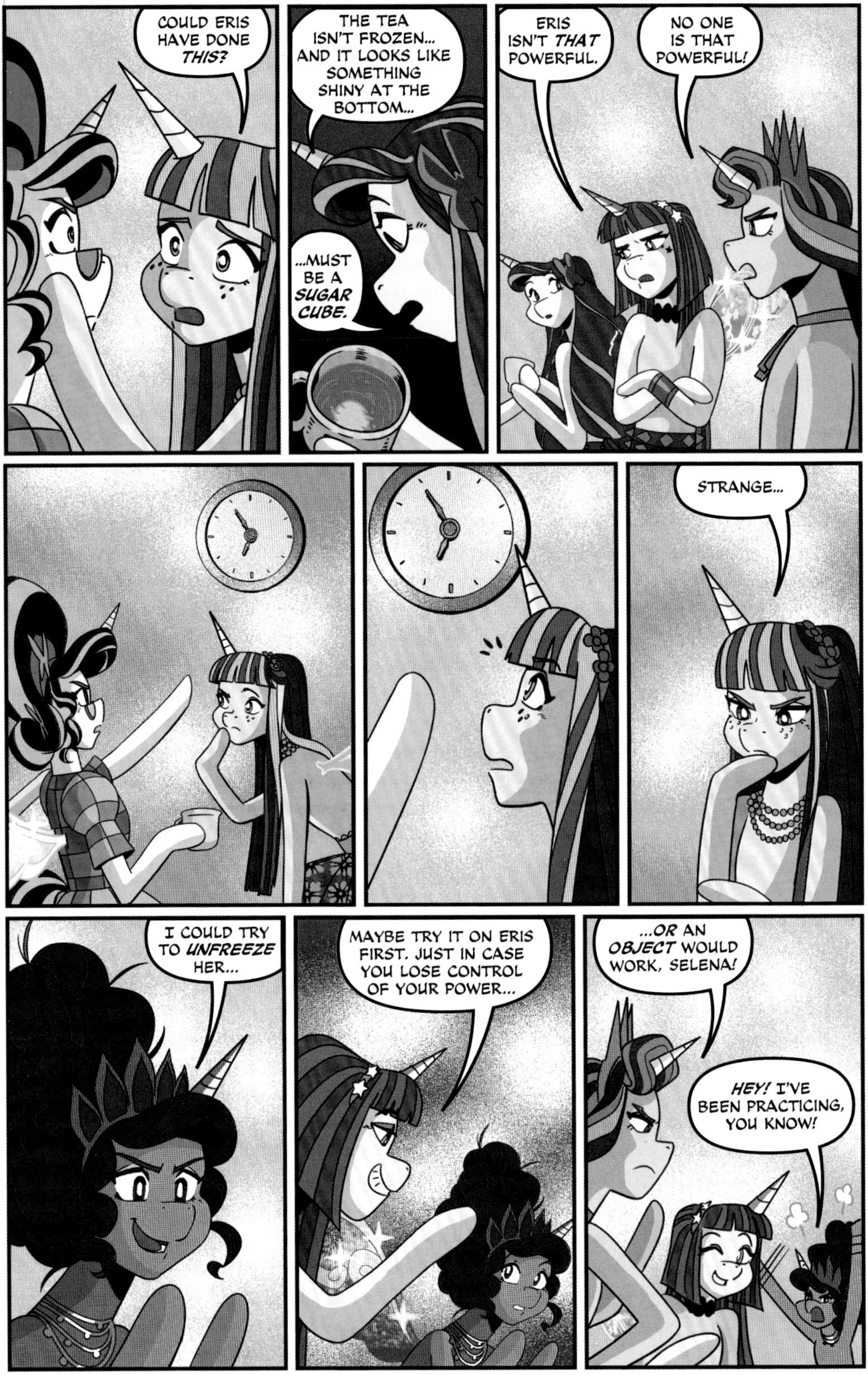
COULD ERIS HAVE DONE *THIS?*
THE TEA ISN'T FROZEN... AND IT LOOKS LIKE SOMETHING SHINY AT THE BOTTOM...
...MUST BE A *SUGAR CUBE.*
ERIS ISN'T *THAT* POWERFUL.
NO ONE IS THAT POWERFUL!
STRANGE...
I COULD TRY TO *UNFREEZE* HER...
MAYBE TRY IT ON ERIS FIRST. JUST IN CASE YOU LOSE CONTROL OF YOUR POWER...
...*OR* AN *OBJECT* WOULD WORK, SELENA!
HEY! I'VE BEEN PRACTICING, YOU KNOW!

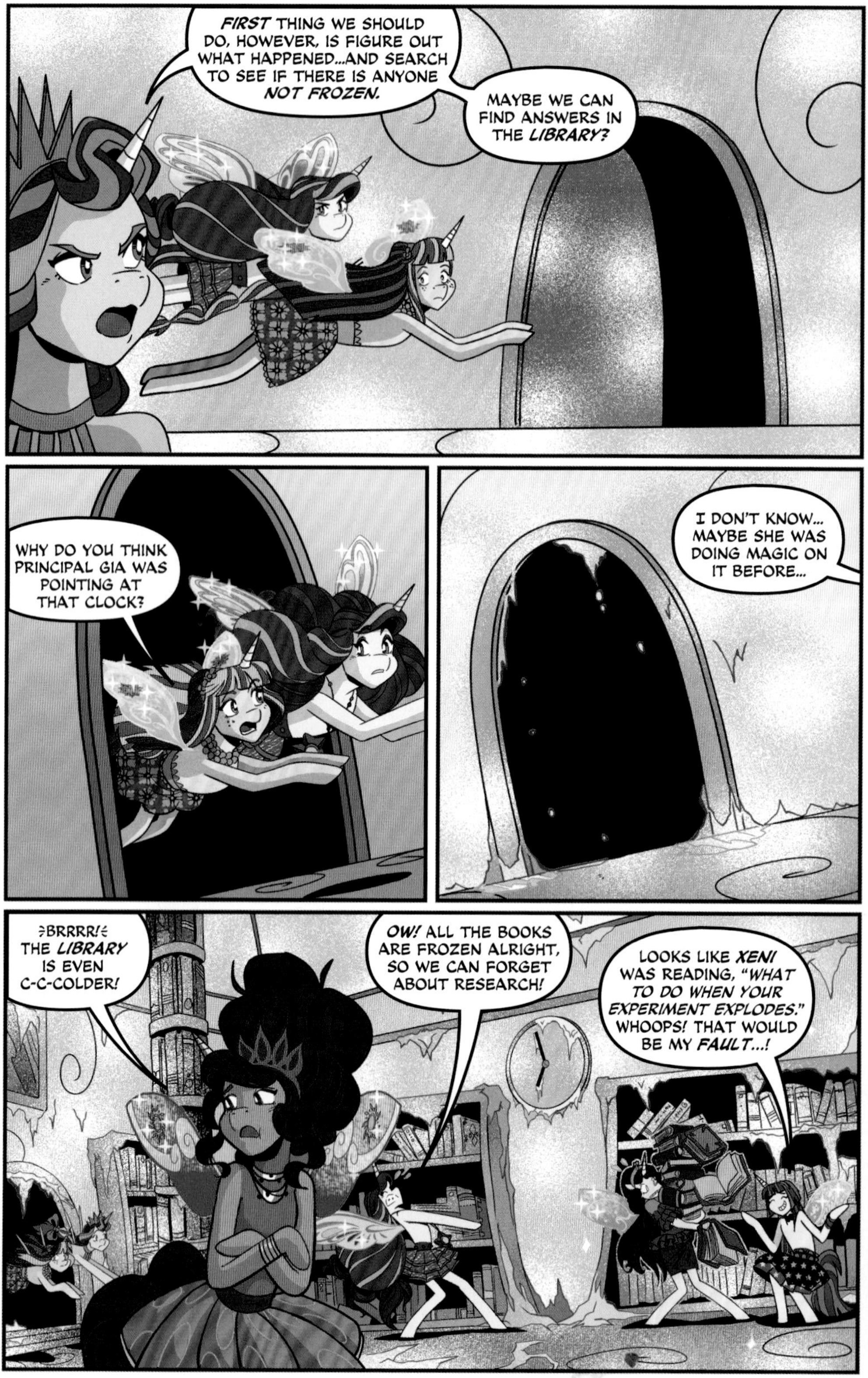
FIRST THING WE SHOULD DO, HOWEVER, IS FIGURE OUT WHAT HAPPENED...AND SEARCH TO SEE IF THERE IS ANYONE NOT FROZEN.
MAYBE WE CAN FIND ANSWERS IN THE LIBRARY?
WHY DO YOU THINK PRINCIPAL GIA WAS POINTING AT THAT CLOCK?
I DON'T KNOW... MAYBE SHE WAS DOING MAGIC ON IT BEFORE...
BRRRR! THE LIBRARY IS EVEN C-C-COLDER!
OW! ALL THE BOOKS ARE FROZEN ALRIGHT, SO WE CAN FORGET ABOUT RESEARCH!
LOOKS LIKE XENI WAS READING, "WHAT TO DO WHEN YOUR EXPERIMENT EXPLODES." WHOOPS! THAT WOULD BE MY FAULT...!

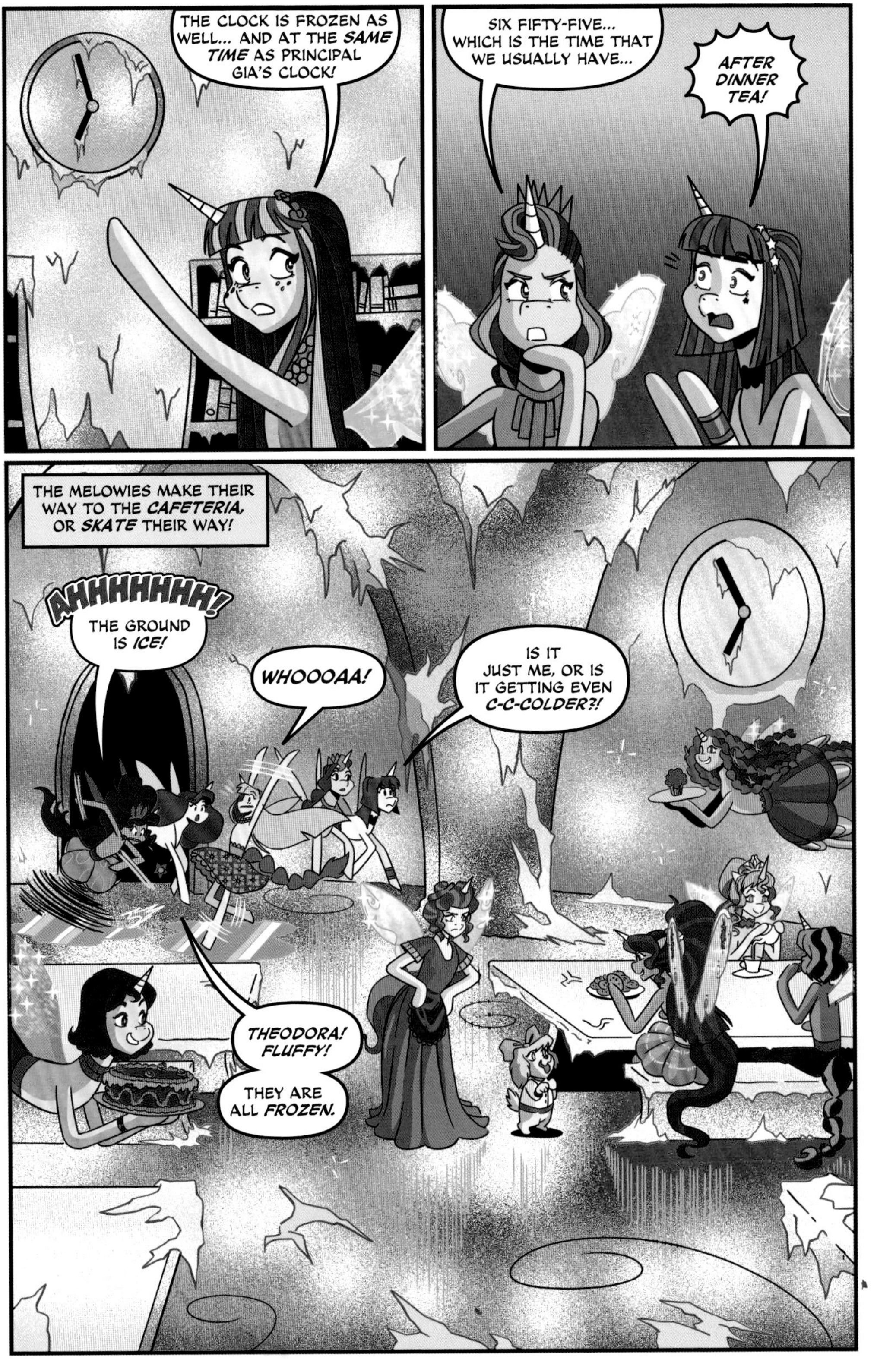
THE CLOCK IS FROZEN AS WELL... AND AT THE SAME TIME AS PRINCIPAL GIA'S CLOCK!
SIX FIFTY-FIVE... WHICH IS THE TIME THAT WE USUALLY HAVE...
AFTER DINNER TEA!
THE MELOWIES MAKE THEIR WAY TO THE CAFETERIA, OR SKATE THEIR WAY!
AHHHHHHH!
THE GROUND IS ICE!
WHOOOAA!
IS IT JUST ME, OR IS IT GETTING EVEN C-C-COLDER?!
THEODORA! FLUFFY!
THEY ARE ALL FROZEN.

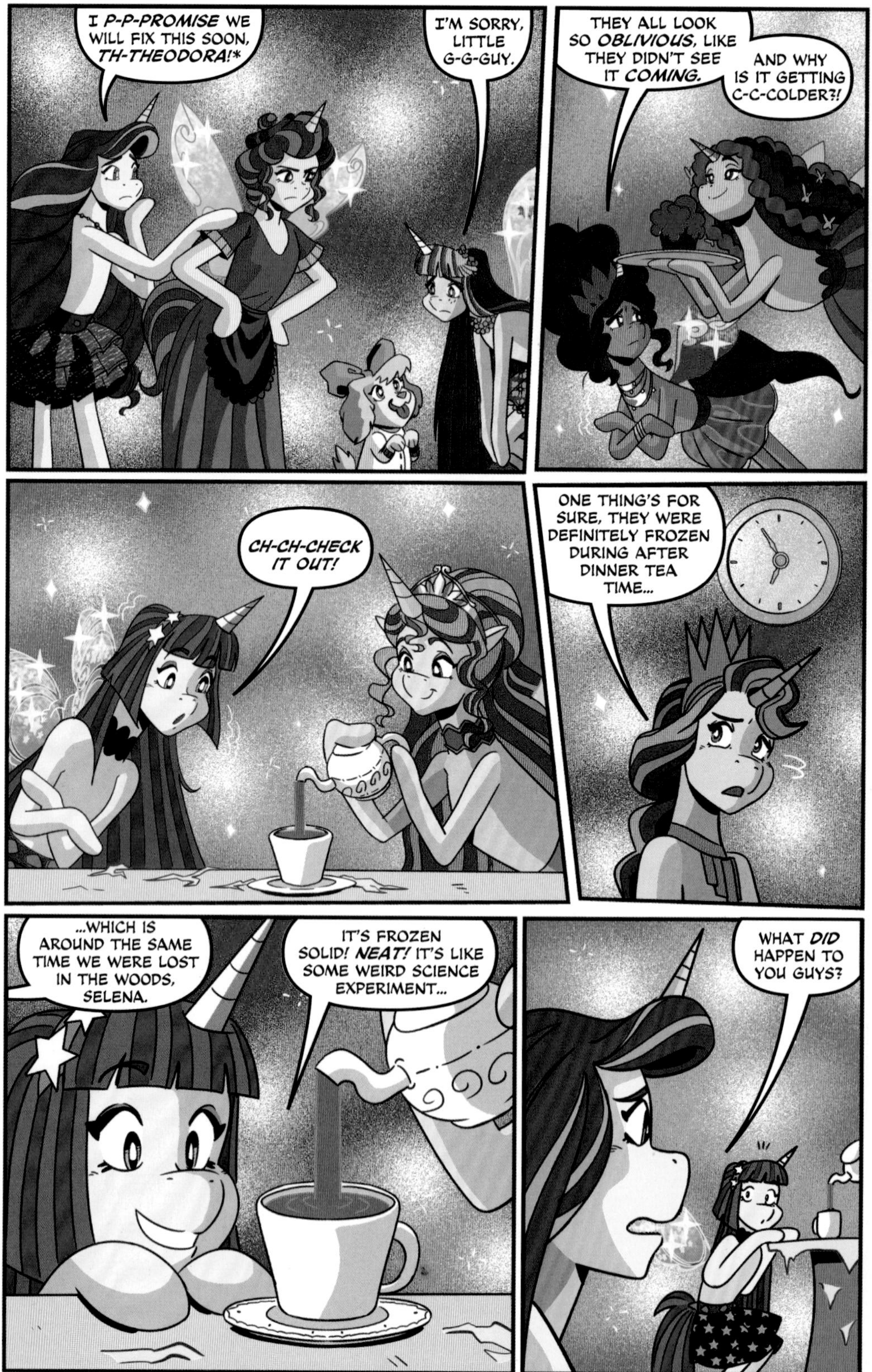
I P-P-PROMISE WE WILL FIX THIS SOON, TH-THEODORA!*
I'M SORRY, LITTLE G-G-GUY.
THEY ALL LOOK SO OBLIVIOUS, LIKE THEY DIDN'T SEE IT COMING.
AND WHY IS IT GETTING C-C-COLDER?!
CH-CH-CHECK IT OUT!
ONE THING'S FOR SURE, THEY WERE DEFINITELY FROZEN DURING AFTER DINNER TEA TIME...
...WHICH IS AROUND THE SAME TIME WE WERE LOST IN THE WOODS, SELENA.
IT'S FROZEN SOLID! NEAT! IT'S LIKE SOME WEIRD SCIENCE EXPERIMENT...
WHAT DID HAPPEN TO YOU GUYS?

*THEODORA, THE SCHOOL COOK, RAISED CLEO SINCE SHE WAS DROPPED OFF AS A BABY, AT DESTINY...WITH THE HELP OF HER DOG, FLUFFY.

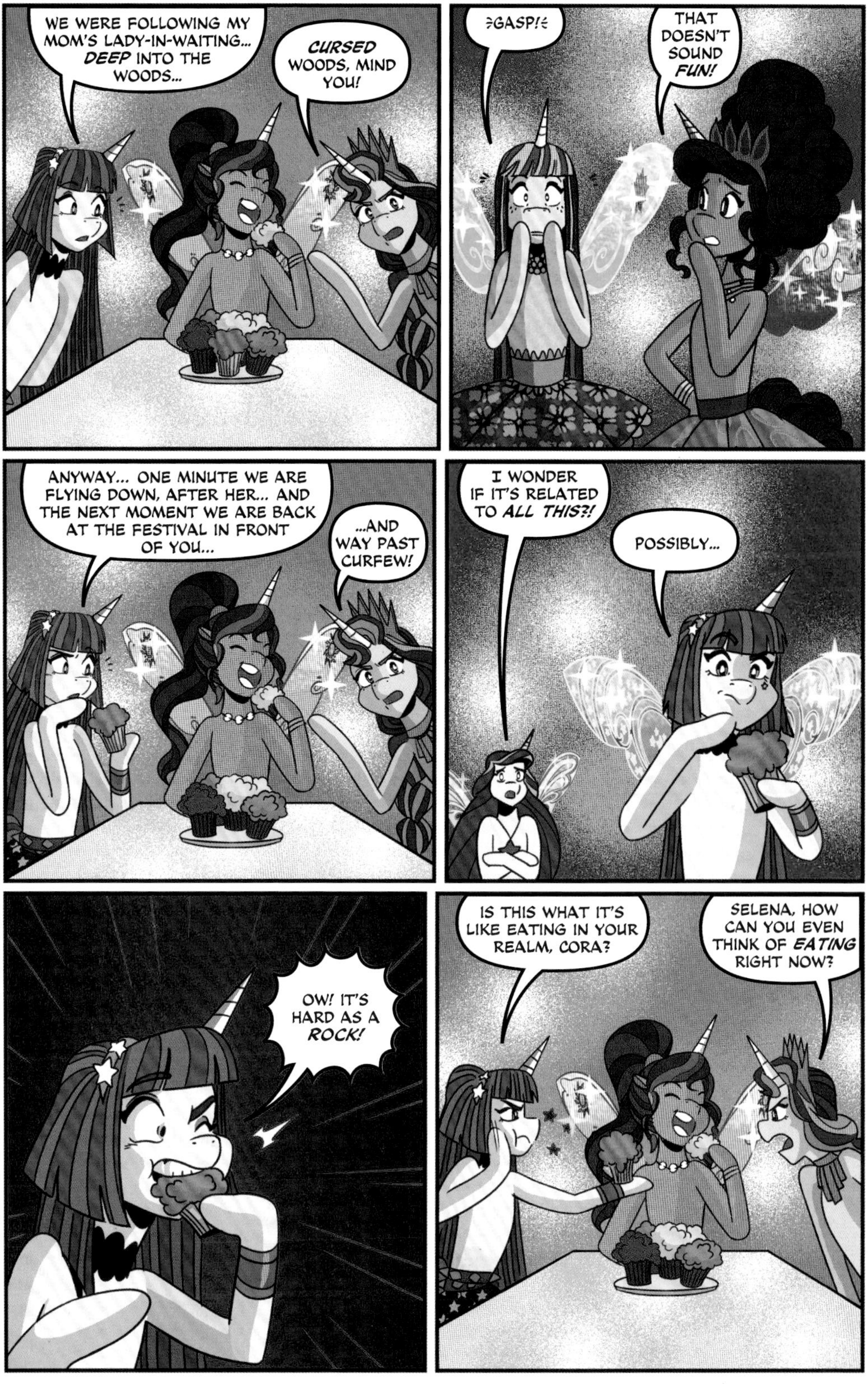
WE WERE FOLLOWING MY MOM'S LADY-IN-WAITING... *DEEP* INTO THE WOODS...
CURSED WOODS, MIND YOU!
⋟GASP!⋞
THAT DOESN'T SOUND *FUN!*
ANYWAY... ONE MINUTE WE ARE FLYING DOWN, AFTER HER... AND THE NEXT MOMENT WE ARE BACK AT THE FESTIVAL IN FRONT OF YOU...
...AND WAY PAST CURFEW!
I WONDER IF IT'S RELATED TO *ALL THIS?!*
POSSIBLY...
OW! IT'S HARD AS A *ROCK!*
IS THIS WHAT IT'S LIKE EATING IN YOUR REALM, CORA?
SELENA, HOW CAN YOU EVEN THINK OF *EATING* RIGHT NOW?

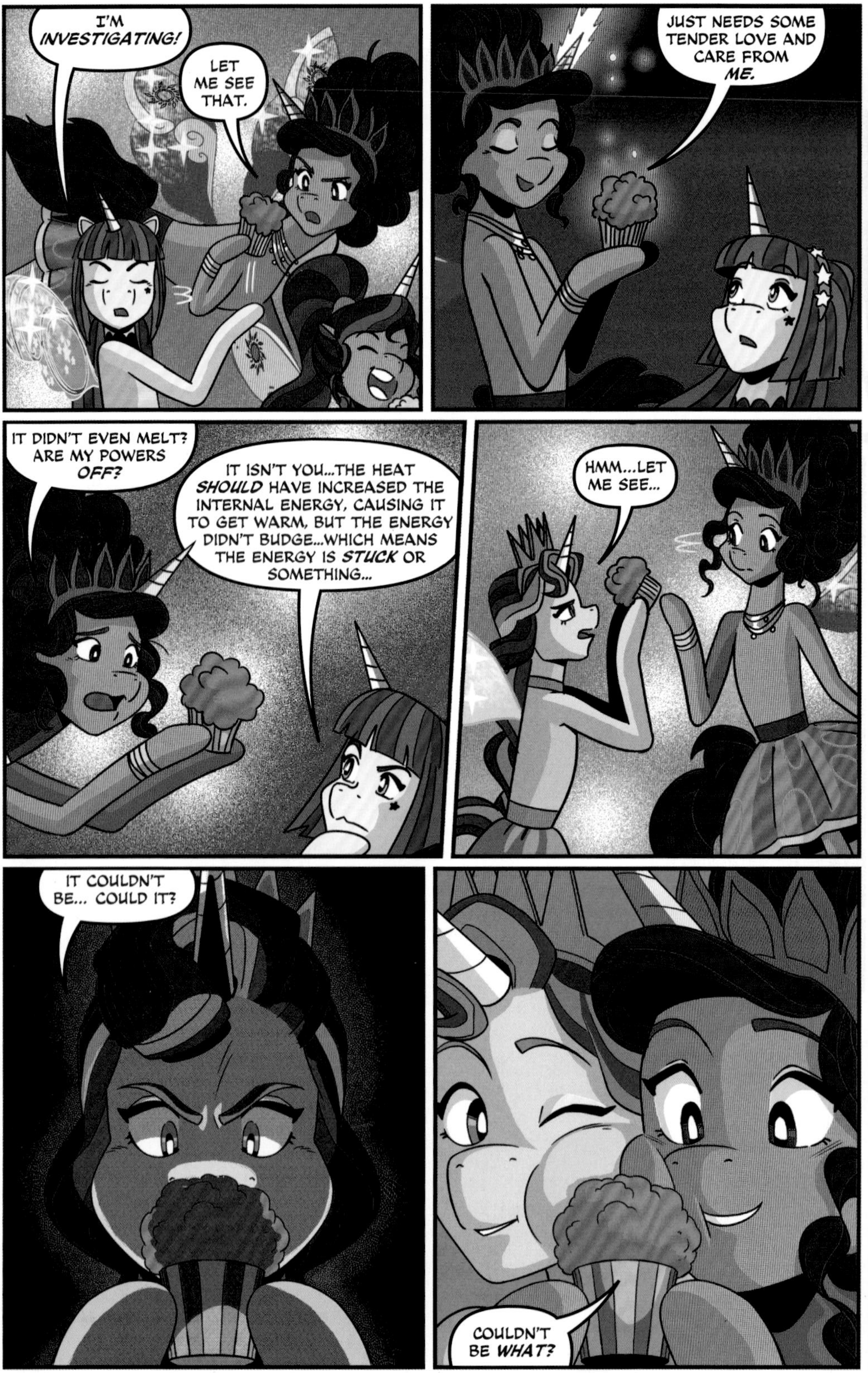
I'M INVESTIGATING!
LET ME SEE THAT.
JUST NEEDS SOME TENDER LOVE AND CARE FROM ME.
IT DIDN'T EVEN MELT? ARE MY POWERS OFF?
IT ISN'T YOU...THE HEAT SHOULD HAVE INCREASED THE INTERNAL ENERGY, CAUSING IT TO GET WARM, BUT THE ENERGY DIDN'T BUDGE...WHICH MEANS THE ENERGY IS STUCK OR SOMETHING...
HMM...LET ME SEE...
IT COULDN'T BE... COULD IT?
COULDN'T BE WHAT?

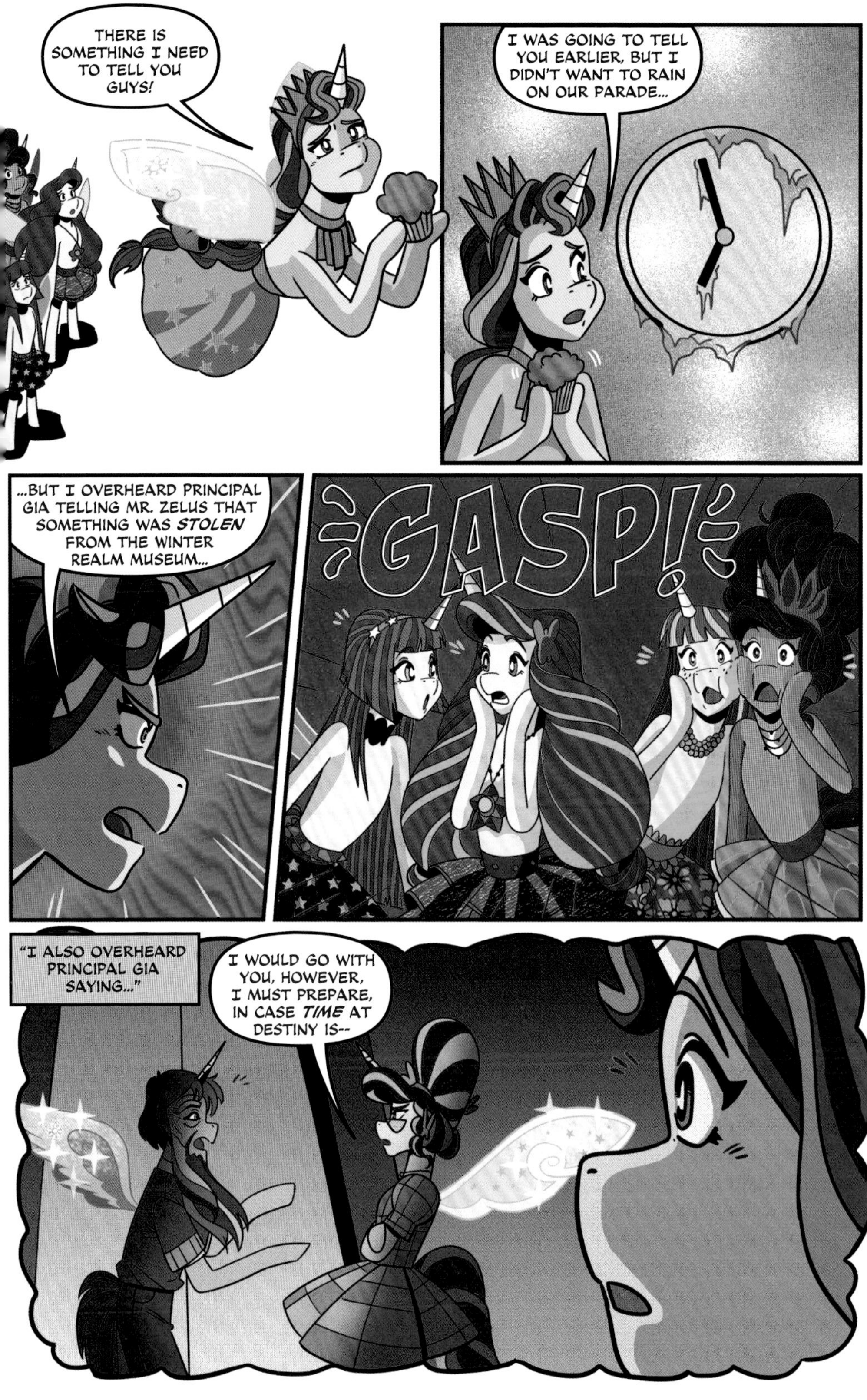
THERE IS SOMETHING I NEED TO TELL YOU GUYS!
I WAS GOING TO TELL YOU EARLIER, BUT I DIDN'T WANT TO RAIN ON OUR PARADE...
...BUT I OVERHEARD PRINCIPAL GIA TELLING MR. ZELUS THAT SOMETHING WAS STOLEN FROM THE WINTER REALM MUSEUM...
GASP!
"I ALSO OVERHEARD PRINCIPAL GIA SAYING..."
I WOULD GO WITH YOU, HOWEVER, I MUST PREPARE, IN CASE TIME AT DESTINY IS--

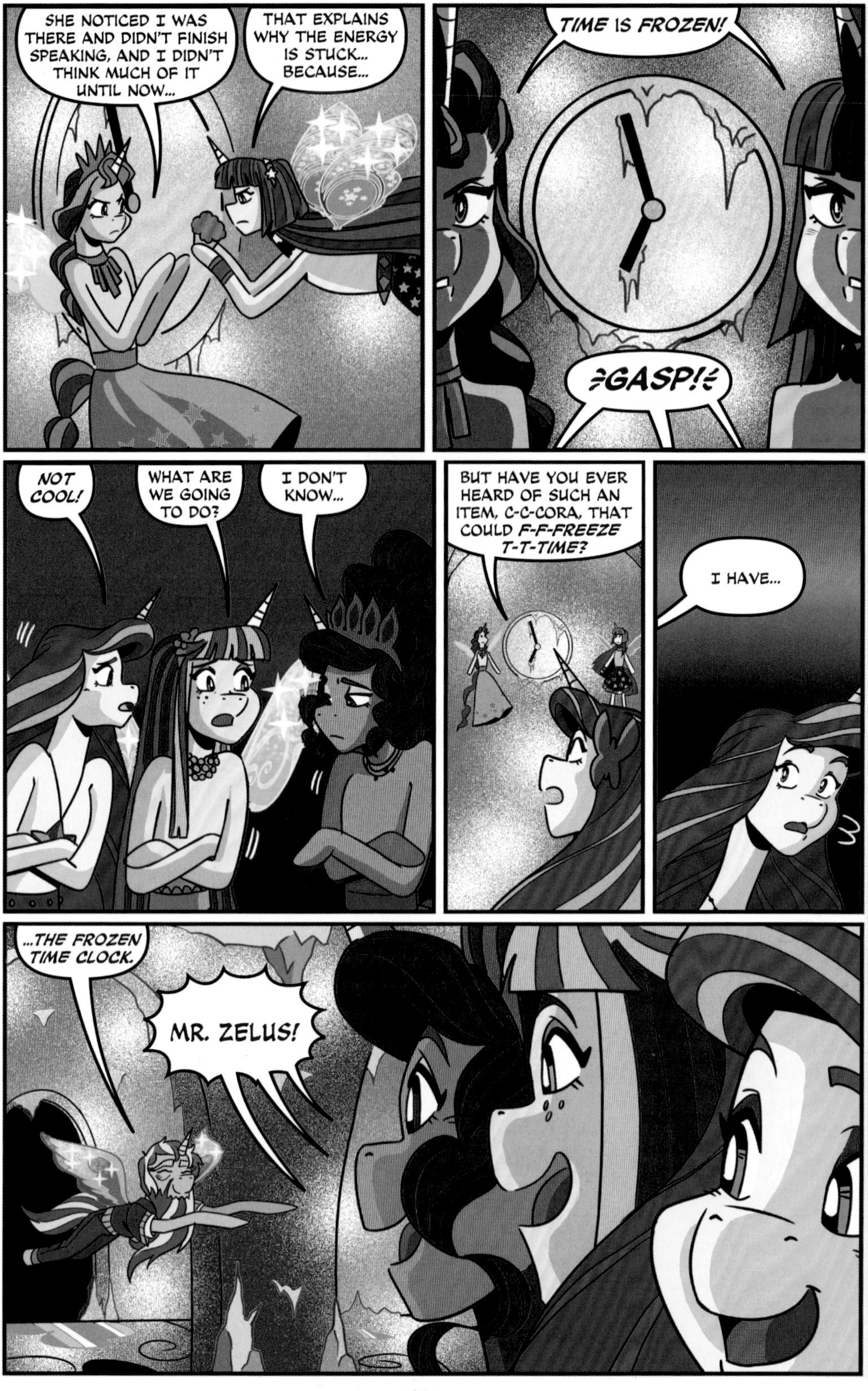
SHE NOTICED I WAS THERE AND DIDN'T FINISH SPEAKING, AND I DIDN'T THINK MUCH OF IT UNTIL NOW...
THAT EXPLAINS WHY THE ENERGY IS STUCK... BECAUSE...
TIME IS FROZEN!
GASP!
NOT COOL!
WHAT ARE WE GOING TO DO?
I DON'T KNOW...
BUT HAVE YOU EVER HEARD OF SUCH AN ITEM, C-C-CORA, THAT COULD F-F-FREEZE T-T-TIME?
I HAVE...
...THE FROZEN TIME CLOCK.
MR. ZELUS!

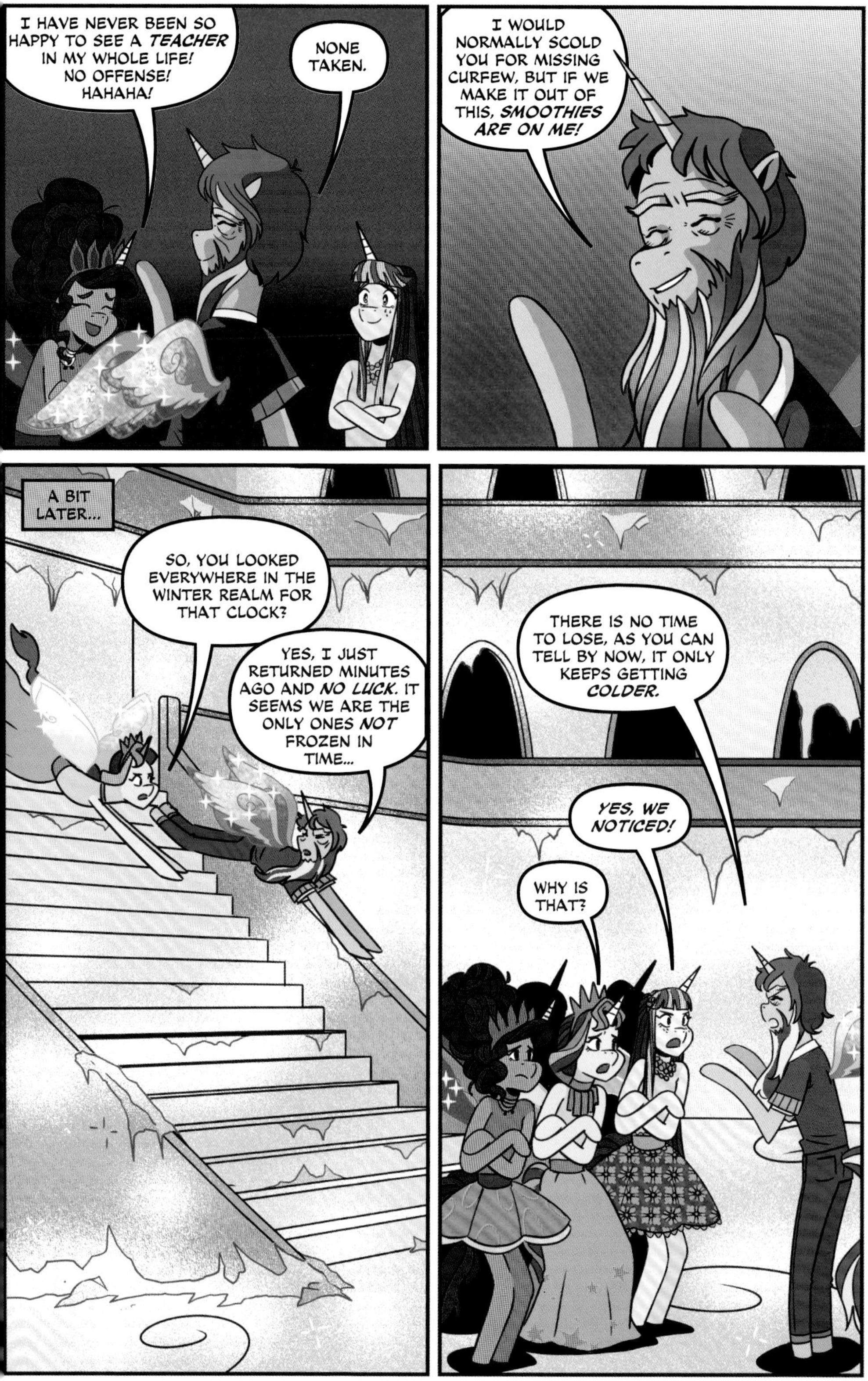

I HAVE NEVER BEEN SO HAPPY TO SEE A *TEACHER* IN MY WHOLE LIFE! NO OFFENSE! HAHAHA!
NONE TAKEN.
I WOULD NORMALLY SCOLD YOU FOR MISSING CURFEW, BUT IF WE MAKE IT OUT OF THIS, *SMOOTHIES ARE ON ME!*
A BIT LATER...
SO, YOU LOOKED EVERYWHERE IN THE WINTER REALM FOR THAT CLOCK?
YES, I JUST RETURNED MINUTES AGO AND *NO LUCK*. IT SEEMS WE ARE THE ONLY ONES *NOT* FROZEN IN TIME...
THERE IS NO TIME TO LOSE, AS YOU CAN TELL BY NOW, IT ONLY KEEPS GETTING *COLDER.*
YES, WE NOTICED!
WHY IS THAT?

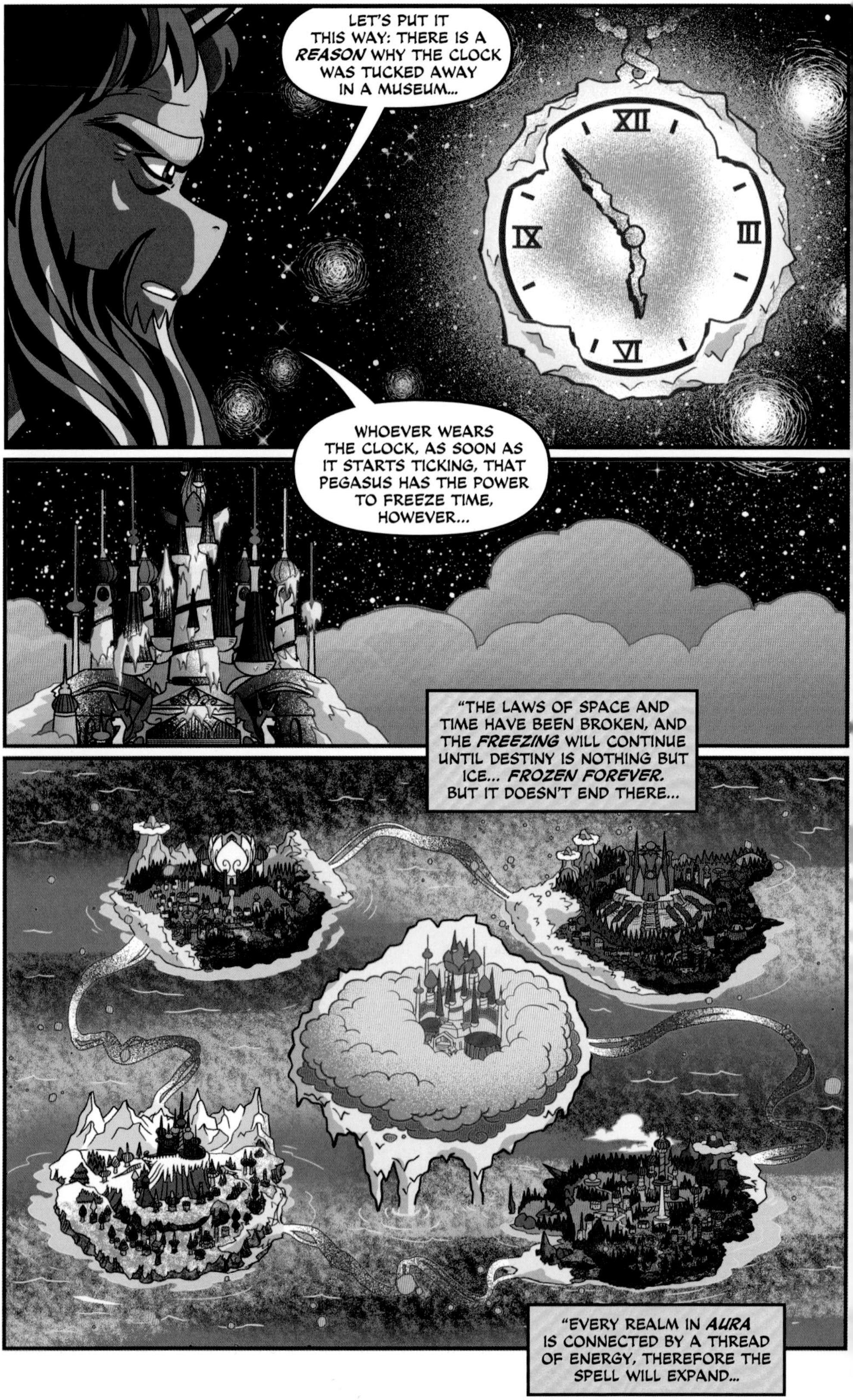
LET'S PUT IT THIS WAY: THERE IS A *REASON* WHY THE CLOCK WAS TUCKED AWAY IN A MUSEUM...
WHOEVER WEARS THE CLOCK, AS SOON AS IT STARTS TICKING, THAT PEGASUS HAS THE POWER TO FREEZE TIME, HOWEVER...
"THE LAWS OF SPACE AND TIME HAVE BEEN BROKEN, AND THE *FREEZING* WILL CONTINUE UNTIL DESTINY IS NOTHING BUT ICE... *FROZEN FOREVER.* BUT IT DOESN'T END THERE...
"EVERY REALM IN *AURA* IS CONNECTED BY A THREAD OF ENERGY, THEREFORE THE SPELL WILL EXPAND...

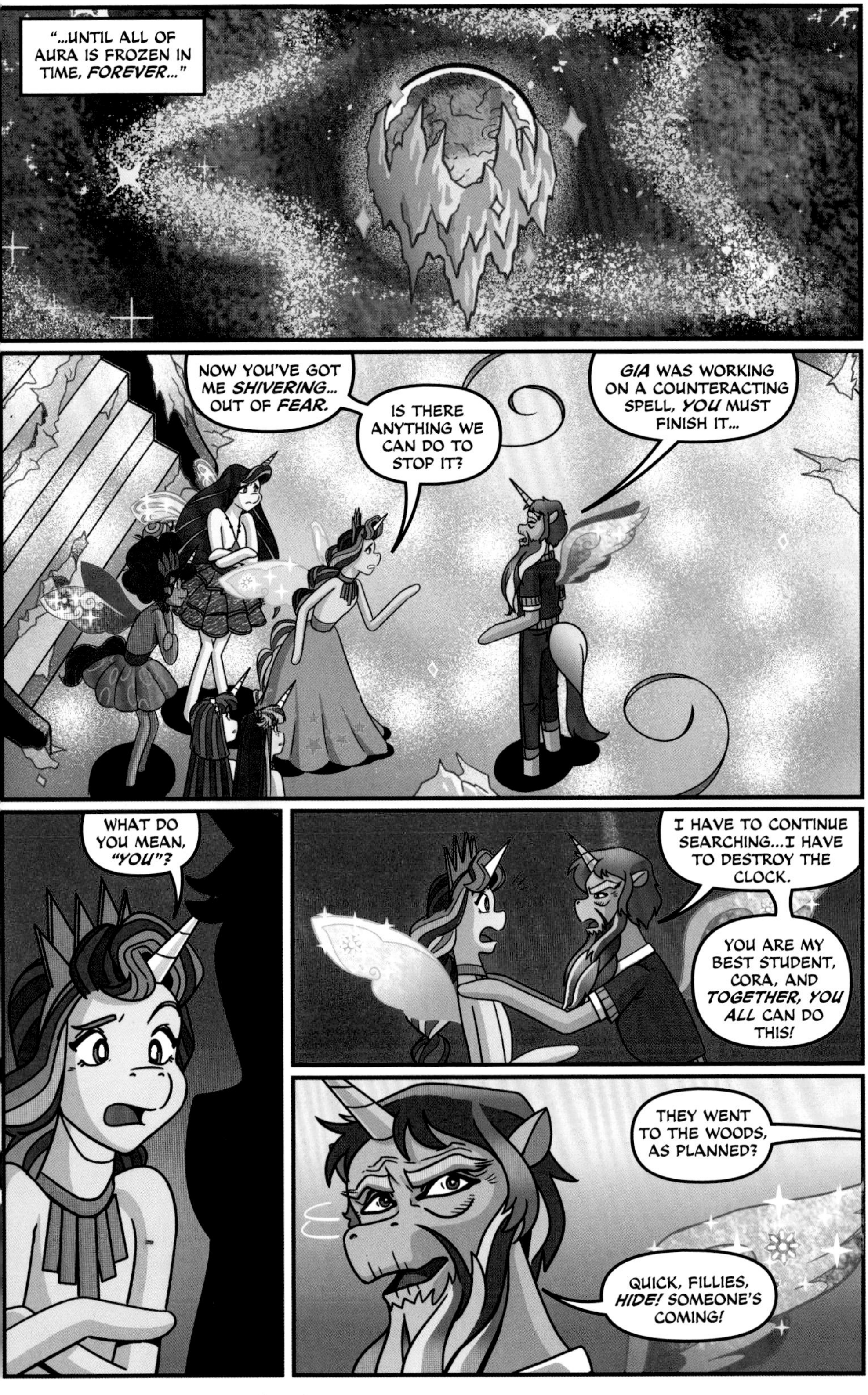
"...UNTIL ALL OF AURA IS FROZEN IN TIME, *FOREVER*..."
NOW YOU'VE GOT ME *SHIVERING*... OUT OF *FEAR*.
IS THERE ANYTHING WE CAN DO TO STOP IT?
GIA WAS WORKING ON A COUNTERACTING SPELL, *YOU* MUST FINISH IT...
WHAT DO YOU MEAN, *"YOU"*?
I HAVE TO CONTINUE SEARCHING...I HAVE TO DESTROY THE CLOCK.
YOU ARE MY BEST STUDENT, CORA, AND *TOGETHER, YOU ALL* CAN DO THIS!
THEY WENT TO THE WOODS, AS PLANNED?
QUICK, FILLIES, *HIDE!* SOMEONE'S COMING!

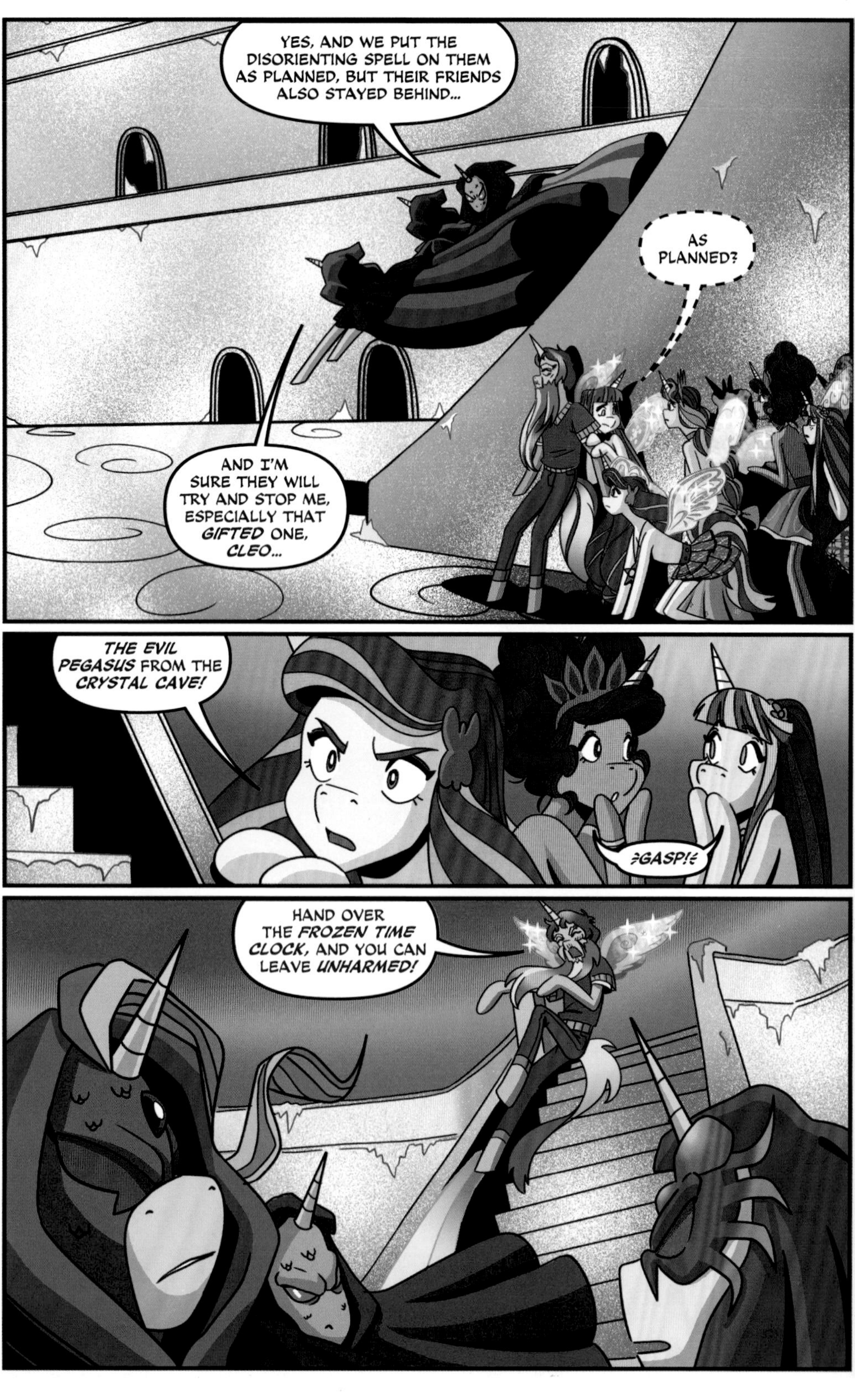
YES, AND WE PUT THE DISORIENTING SPELL ON THEM AS PLANNED, BUT THEIR FRIENDS ALSO STAYED BEHIND...
AS PLANNED?
AND I'M SURE THEY WILL TRY AND STOP ME, ESPECIALLY THAT GIFTED ONE, CLEO...
THE EVIL PEGASUS FROM THE CRYSTAL CAVE!
GASP!
HAND OVER THE FROZEN TIME CLOCK, AND YOU CAN LEAVE UNHARMED!

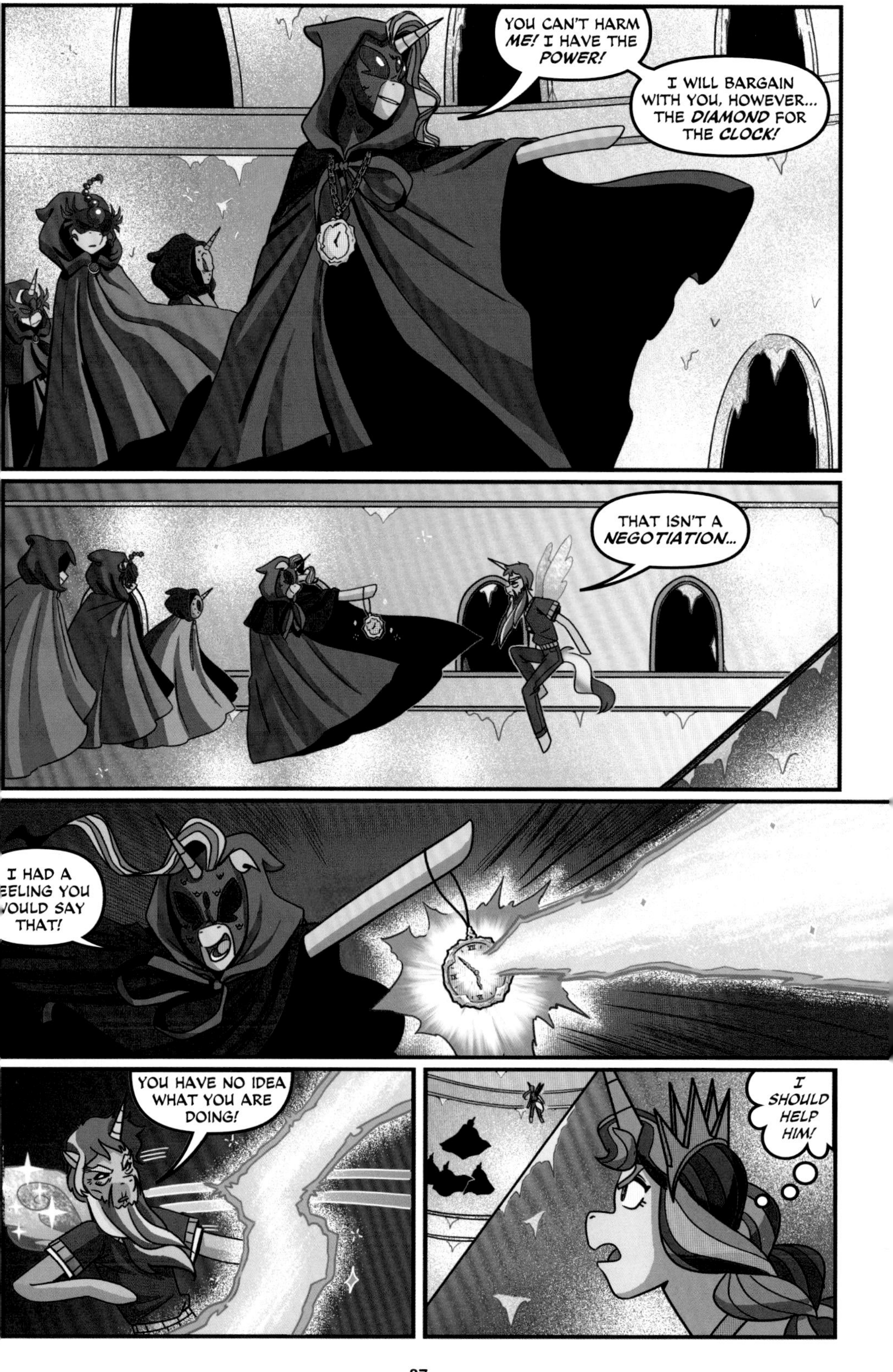
YOU CAN'T HARM ME! I HAVE THE POWER!
I WILL BARGAIN WITH YOU, HOWEVER... THE DIAMOND FOR THE CLOCK!
THAT ISN'T A NEGOTIATION...
I HAD A EELING YOU OULD SAY THAT!
YOU HAVE NO IDEA WHAT YOU ARE DOING!
I SHOULD HELP HIM!

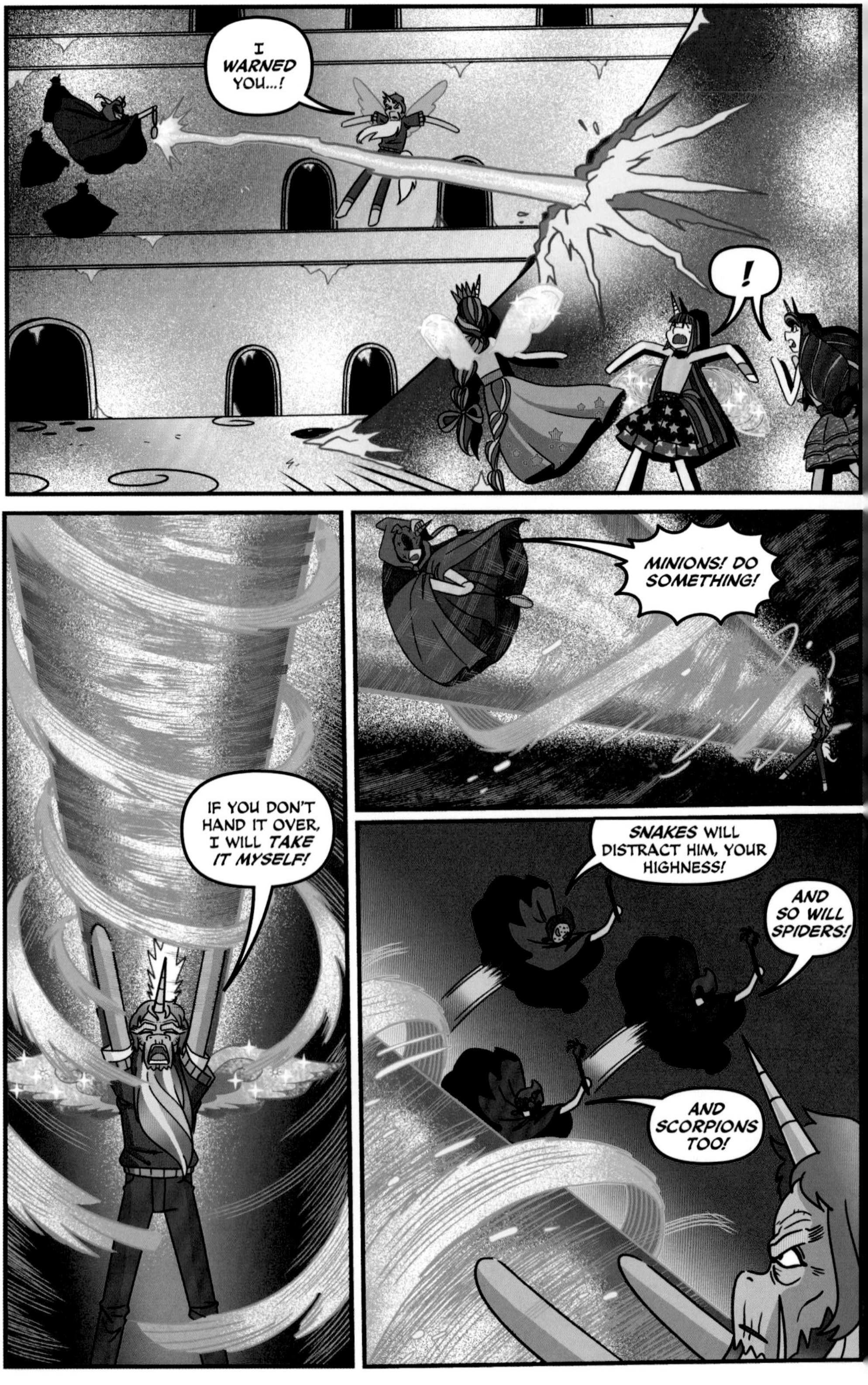
I WARNED YOU...!
!
MINIONS! DO SOMETHING!
IF YOU DON'T HAND IT OVER, I WILL TAKE IT MYSELF!
SNAKES WILL DISTRACT HIM, YOUR HIGHNESS!
AND SO WILL SPIDERS!
AND SCORPIONS TOO!

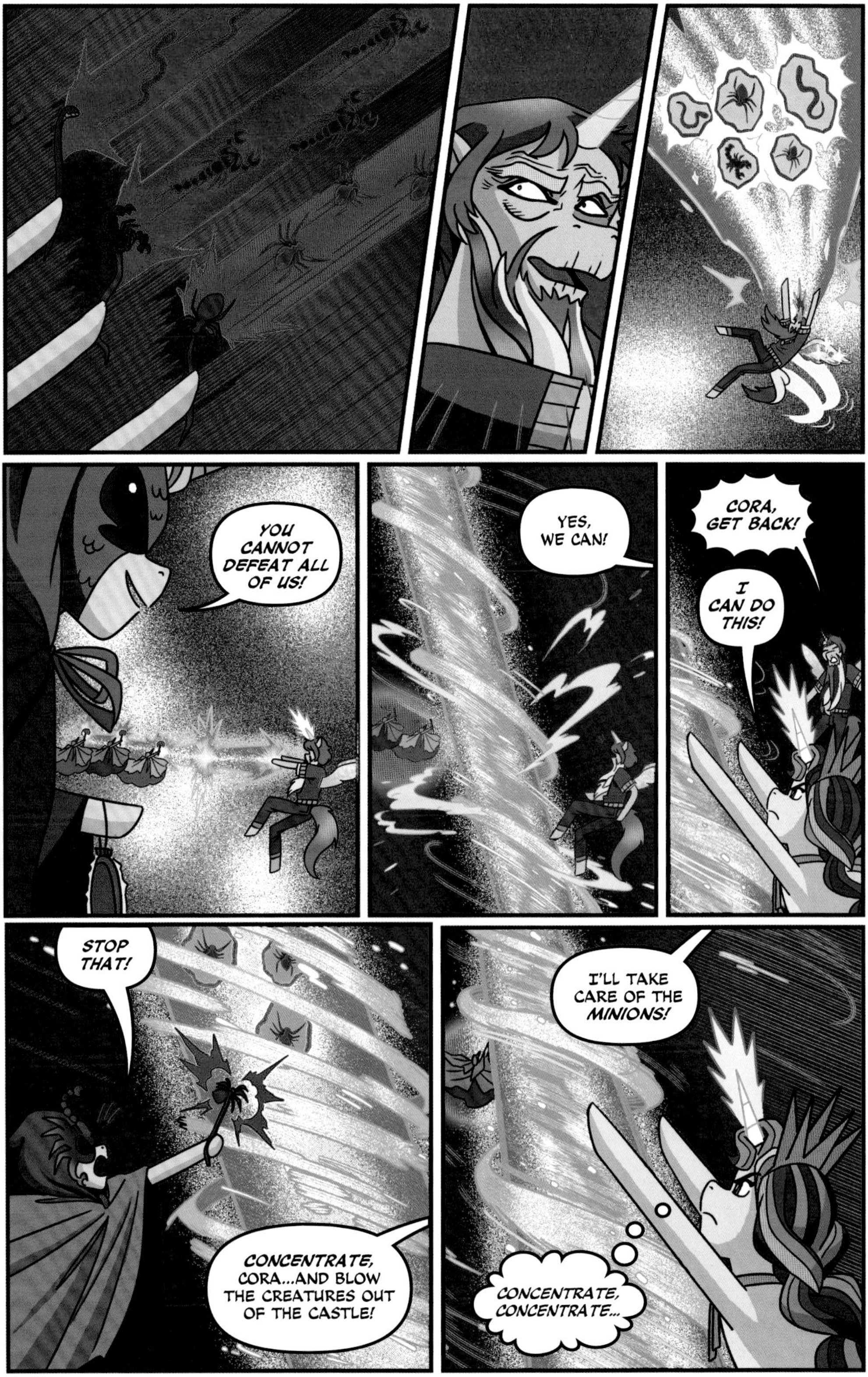
YOU CANNOT DEFEAT ALL OF US!
YES, WE CAN!
CORA, GET BACK!
I CAN DO THIS!
STOP THAT!
CONCENTRATE, CORA...AND BLOW THE CREATURES OUT OF THE CASTLE!
I'LL TAKE CARE OF THE MINIONS!
CONCENTRATE, CONCENTRATE...

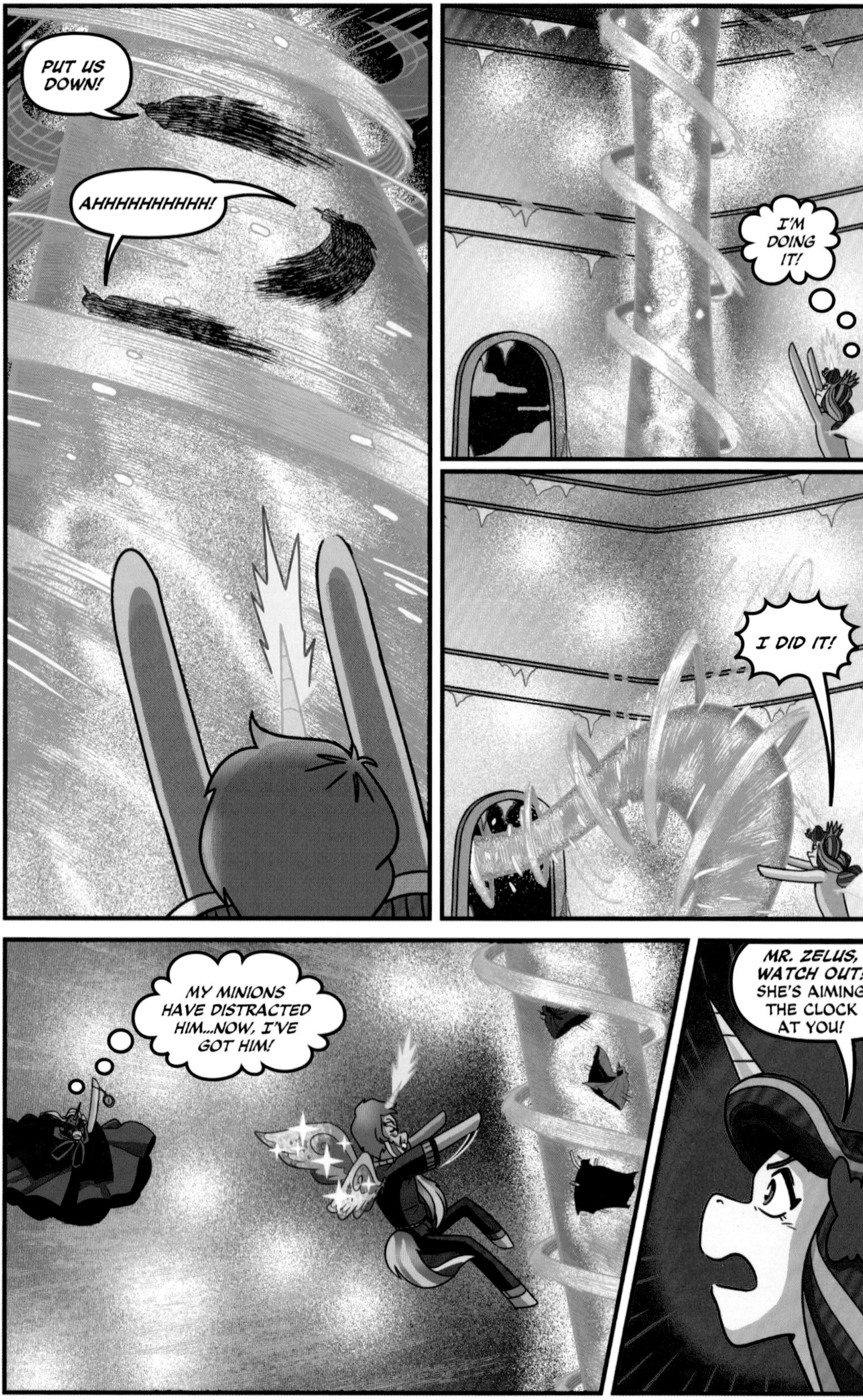
PUT US DOWN!
AHHHHHHHHHH!
I'M DOING IT!
I DID IT!
MY MINIONS HAVE DISTRACTED HIM...NOW, I'VE GOT HIM!
MR. ZELUS, WATCH OUT! SHE'S AIMING THE CLOCK AT YOU!

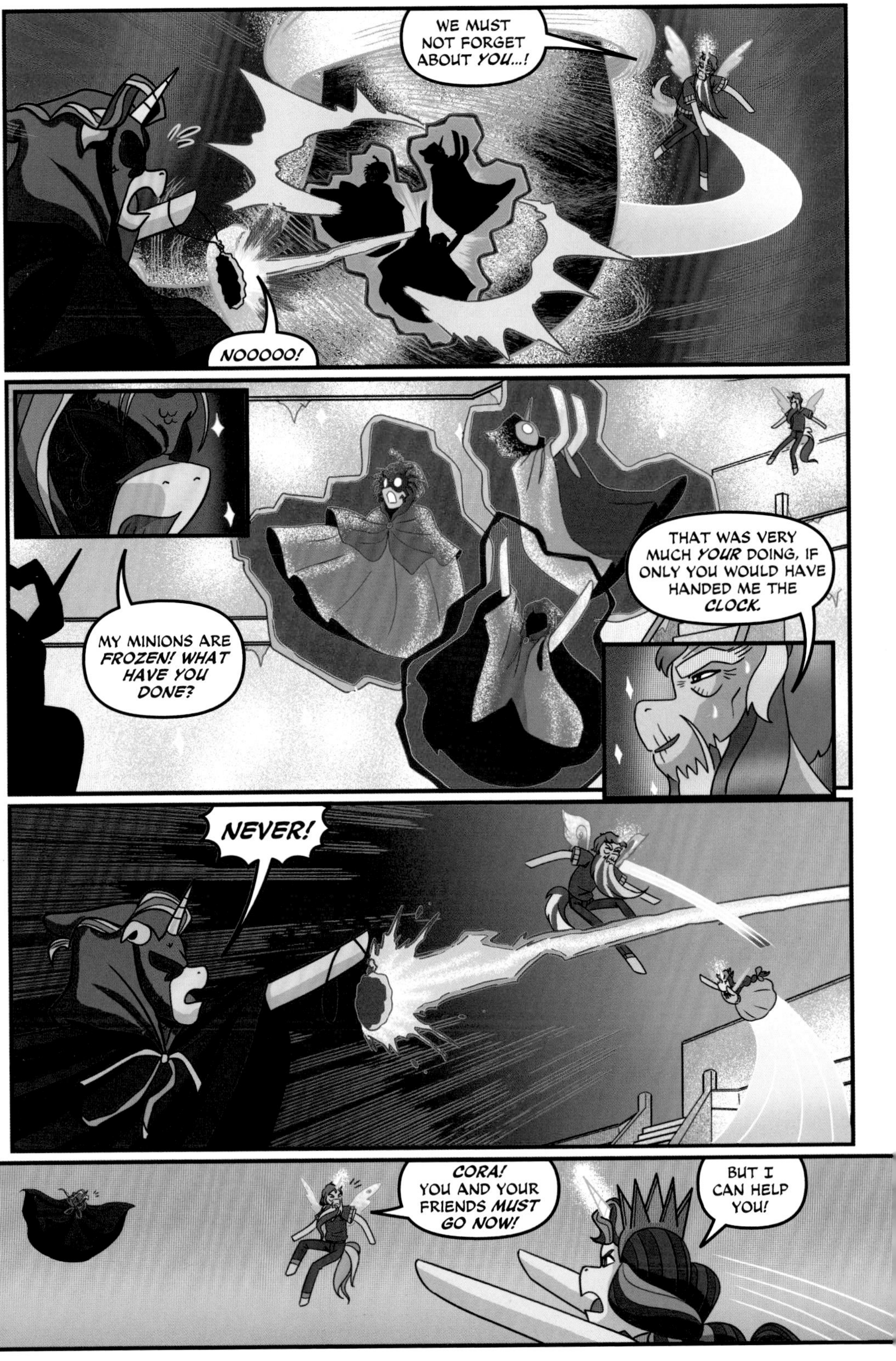
WE MUST NOT FORGET ABOUT YOU...!
NOOOOO!
MY MINIONS ARE FROZEN! WHAT HAVE YOU DONE?
THAT WAS VERY MUCH YOUR DOING, IF ONLY YOU WOULD HAVE HANDED ME THE CLOCK.
NEVER!
CORA! YOU AND YOUR FRIENDS MUST GO NOW!
BUT I CAN HELP YOU!

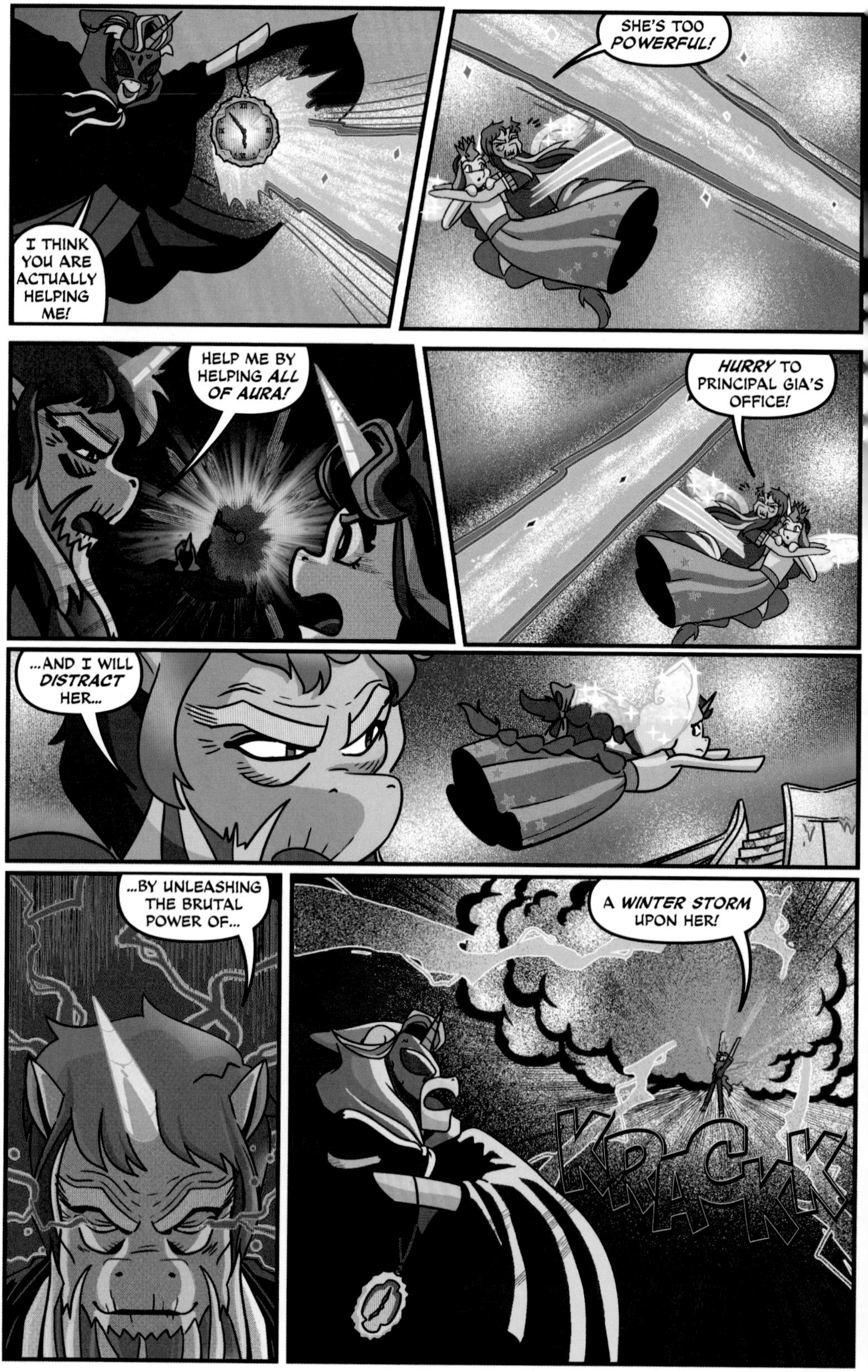
I THINK YOU ARE ACTUALLY HELPING ME!
SHE'S TOO POWERFUL!
HELP ME BY HELPING ALL OF AURA!
HURRY TO PRINCIPAL GIA'S OFFICE!
...AND I WILL DISTRACT HER...
...BY UNLEASHING THE BRUTAL POWER OF...
A WINTER STORM UPON HER!
KRACK

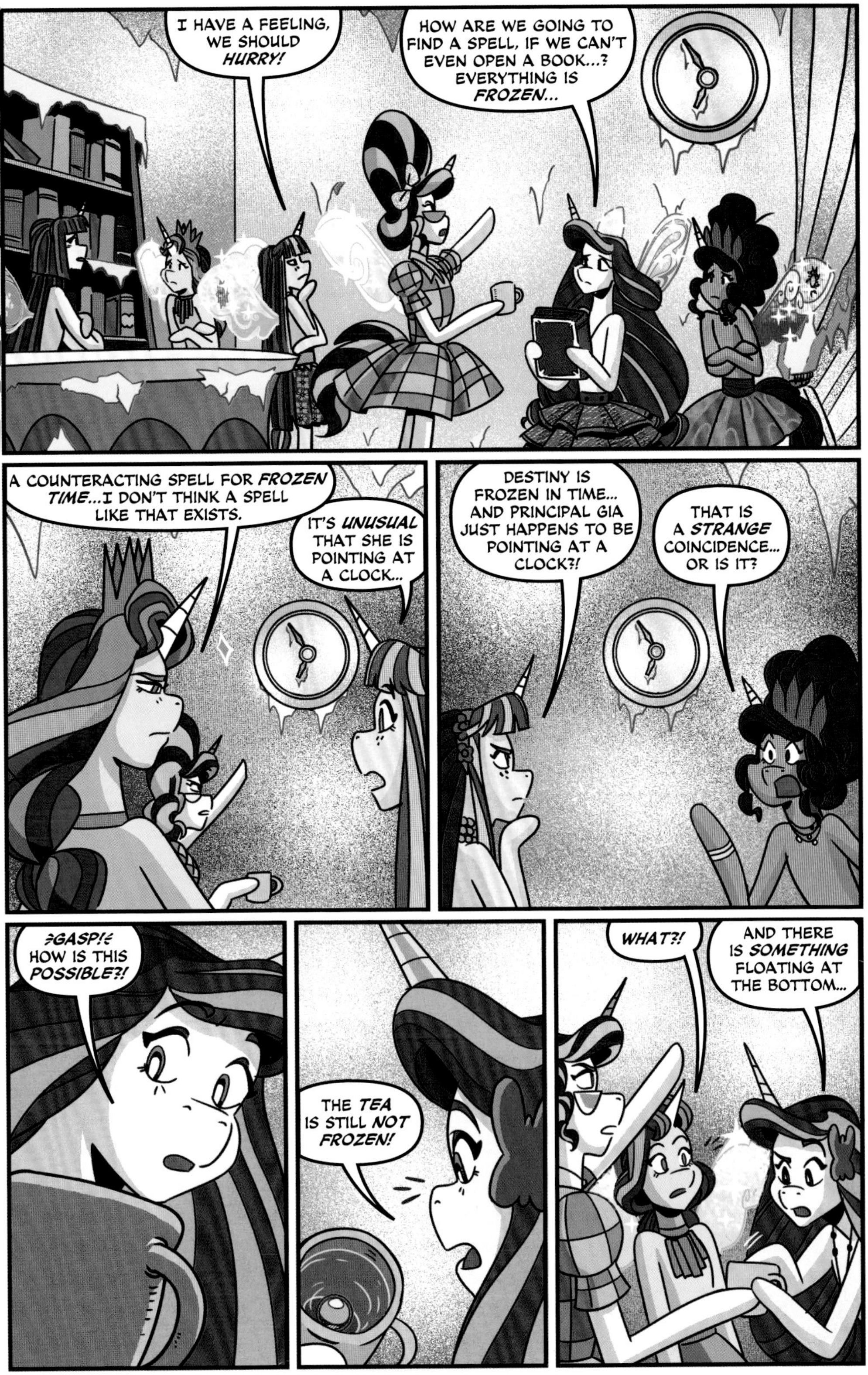

I HAVE A FEELING, WE SHOULD HURRY!
HOW ARE WE GOING TO FIND A SPELL, IF WE CAN'T EVEN OPEN A BOOK...? EVERYTHING IS FROZEN...
A COUNTERACTING SPELL FOR FROZEN TIME...I DON'T THINK A SPELL LIKE THAT EXISTS.
IT'S UNUSUAL THAT SHE IS POINTING AT A CLOCK...
DESTINY IS FROZEN IN TIME... AND PRINCIPAL GIA JUST HAPPENS TO BE POINTING AT A CLOCK?!
THAT IS A STRANGE COINCIDENCE... OR IS IT?
GASP! HOW IS THIS POSSIBLE?!
THE TEA IS STILL NOT FROZEN!
WHAT?!
AND THERE IS SOMETHING FLOATING AT THE BOTTOM...

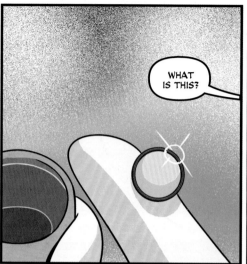

WHAT IS THIS?

IT MUST HAVE KEPT THE TEA FROM FREEZING...

I BET SHE THREW IT IN HER TEACUP BEFORE SHE FROZE...

WHAT'S THIS...?

THERE'S A SMALL OPENING AROUND THE MIDDLE, I DIDN'T NOTICE BEFORE...

LET'S PLACE IT IN THE CLOCK AND SEE WHAT HAPPENS...?

SOMETHING IS DEFINITELY HAPPENING!

BE CAREFUL, GUYS...! MAYBE STAND AWAY FROM THE--

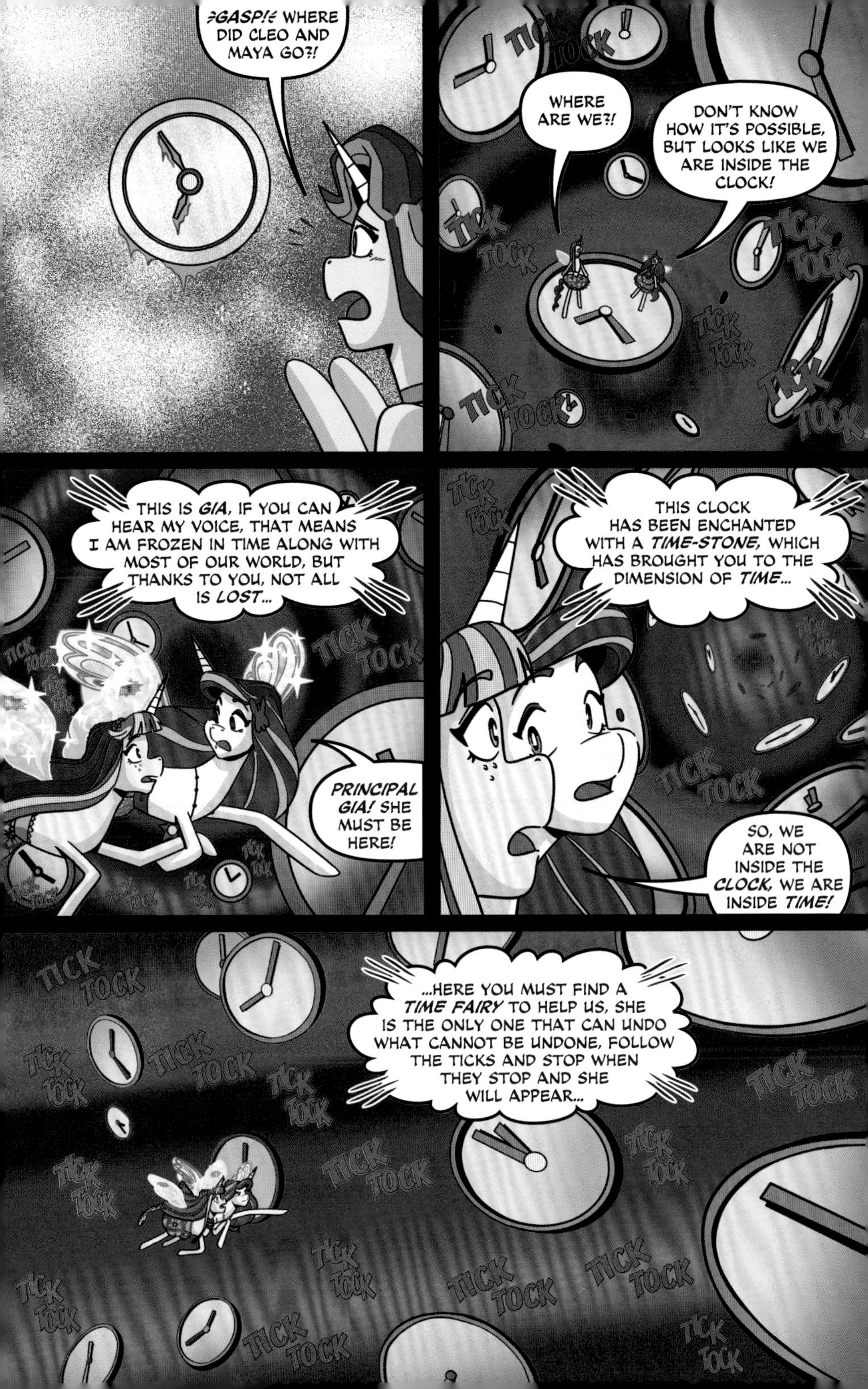

GASP! WHERE DID CLEO AND MAYA GO?!
WHERE ARE WE?!
DON'T KNOW HOW IT'S POSSIBLE, BUT LOOKS LIKE WE ARE INSIDE THE CLOCK!
TICK TOCK
THIS IS GIA, IF YOU CAN HEAR MY VOICE, THAT MEANS I AM FROZEN IN TIME ALONG WITH MOST OF OUR WORLD, BUT THANKS TO YOU, NOT ALL IS LOST...
PRINCIPAL GIA! SHE MUST BE HERE!
TICK TOCK
THIS CLOCK HAS BEEN ENCHANTED WITH A TIME-STONE, WHICH HAS BROUGHT YOU TO THE DIMENSION OF TIME...
SO, WE ARE NOT INSIDE THE CLOCK, WE ARE INSIDE TIME!
TICK TOCK
...HERE YOU MUST FIND A TIME FAIRY TO HELP US, SHE IS THE ONLY ONE THAT CAN UNDO WHAT CANNOT BE UNDONE, FOLLOW THE TICKS AND STOP WHEN THEY STOP AND SHE WILL APPEAR...
TICK TOCK

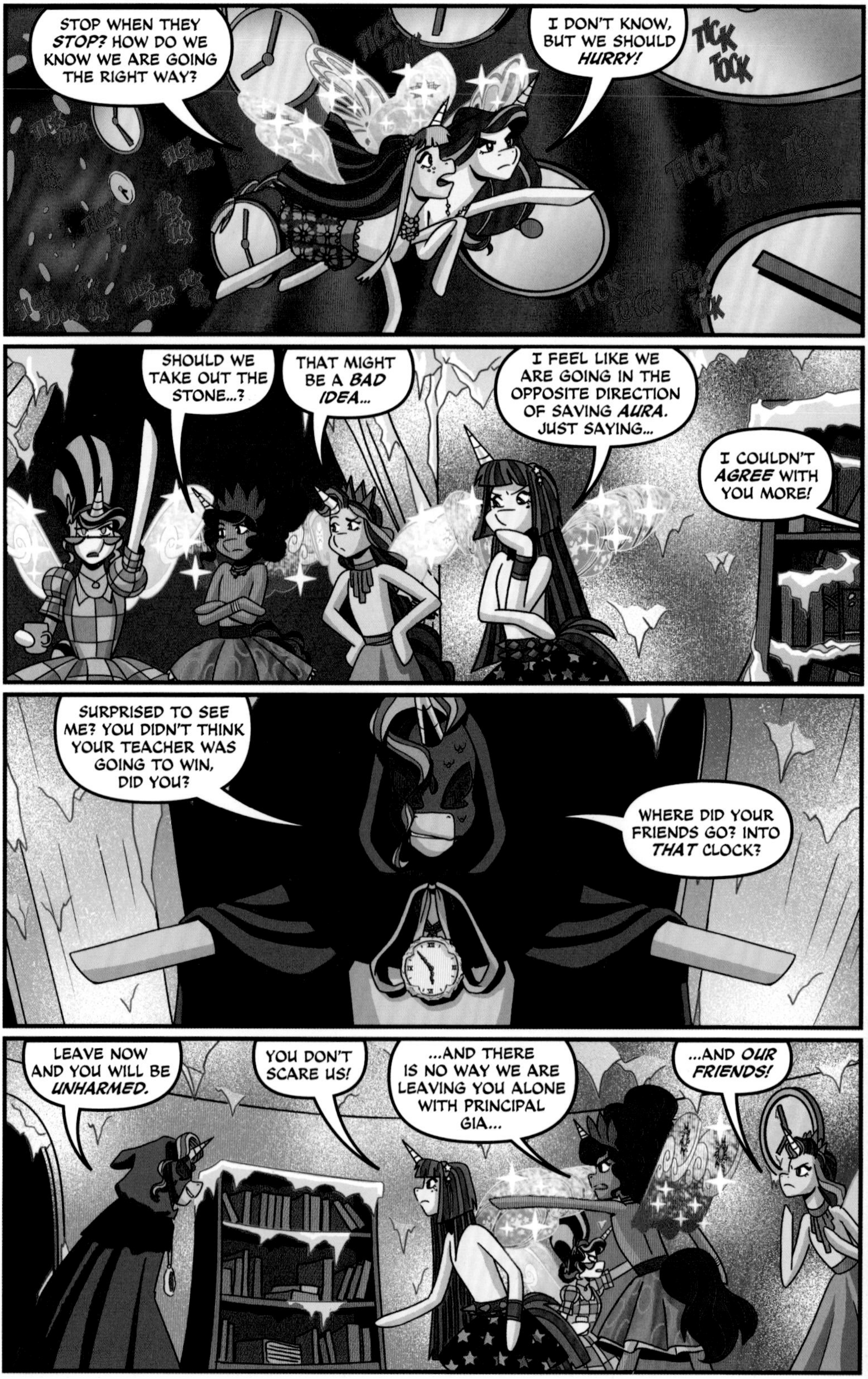
STOP WHEN THEY *STOP?* HOW DO WE KNOW WE ARE GOING THE RIGHT WAY?
I DON'T KNOW, BUT WE SHOULD *HURRY!*
TICK TOCK
SHOULD WE TAKE OUT THE STONE...?
THAT MIGHT BE A *BAD IDEA*...
I FEEL LIKE WE ARE GOING IN THE OPPOSITE DIRECTION OF SAVING *AURA*. JUST SAYING...
I COULDN'T *AGREE* WITH YOU MORE!
SURPRISED TO SEE ME? YOU DIDN'T THINK YOUR TEACHER WAS GOING TO WIN, DID YOU?
WHERE DID YOUR FRIENDS GO? INTO *THAT* CLOCK?
LEAVE NOW AND YOU WILL BE *UNHARMED.*
YOU DON'T SCARE US!
...AND THERE IS NO WAY WE ARE LEAVING YOU ALONE WITH PRINCIPAL GIA...
...AND *OUR FRIENDS!*

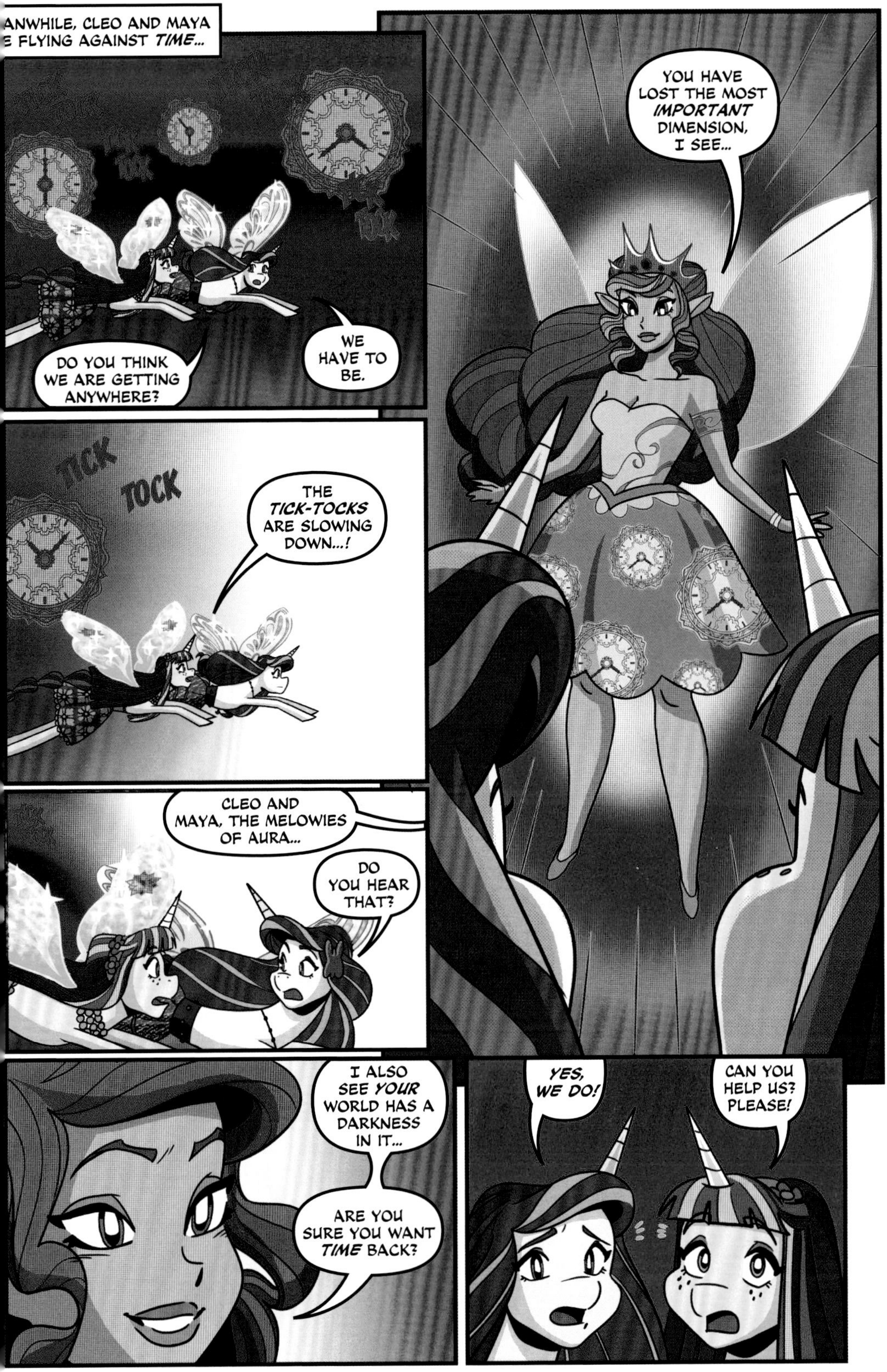
ANWHILE, CLEO AND MAYA
E FLYING AGAINST *TIME*...
TICK
TOCK
TICK
TOCK
DO YOU THINK WE ARE GETTING ANYWHERE?
WE HAVE TO BE.
YOU HAVE LOST THE MOST *IMPORTANT* DIMENSION, I SEE...
TICK
TOCK
THE *TICK-TOCKS* ARE SLOWING DOWN...!
CLEO AND MAYA, THE MELOWIES OF AURA...
DO YOU HEAR THAT?
I ALSO SEE *YOUR* WORLD HAS A DARKNESS IN IT...
ARE YOU SURE YOU WANT *TIME* BACK?
YES, WE DO!
CAN YOU HELP US? PLEASE!

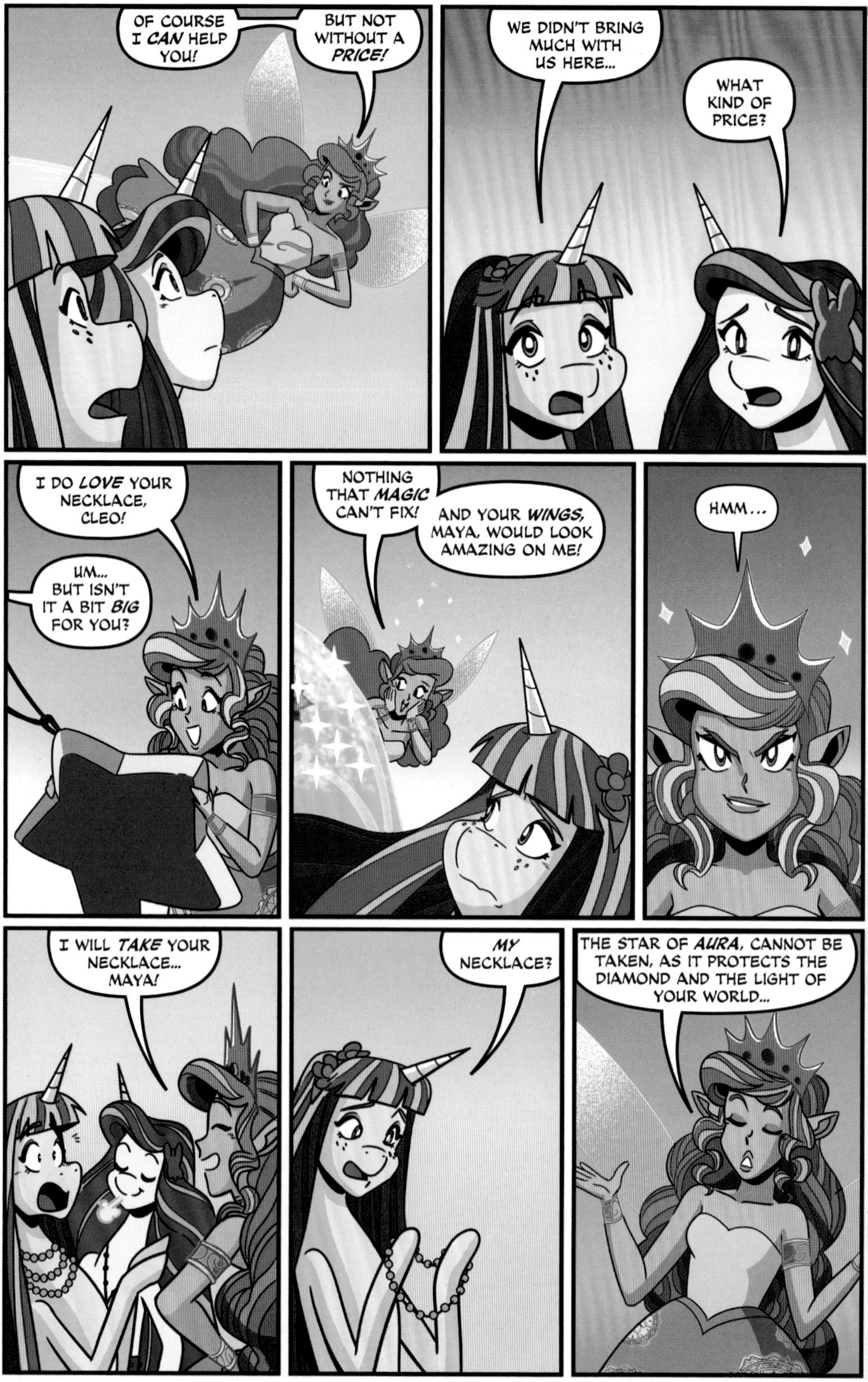
OF COURSE I CAN HELP YOU!
BUT NOT WITHOUT A PRICE!
WE DIDN'T BRING MUCH WITH US HERE...
WHAT KIND OF PRICE?
I DO LOVE YOUR NECKLACE, CLEO!
UM... BUT ISN'T IT A BIT BIG FOR YOU?
NOTHING THAT MAGIC CAN'T FIX!
AND YOUR WINGS, MAYA, WOULD LOOK AMAZING ON ME!
HMM...
I WILL TAKE YOUR NECKLACE... MAYA!
MY NECKLACE?
THE STAR OF AURA, CANNOT BE TAKEN, AS IT PROTECTS THE DIAMOND AND THE LIGHT OF YOUR WORLD...

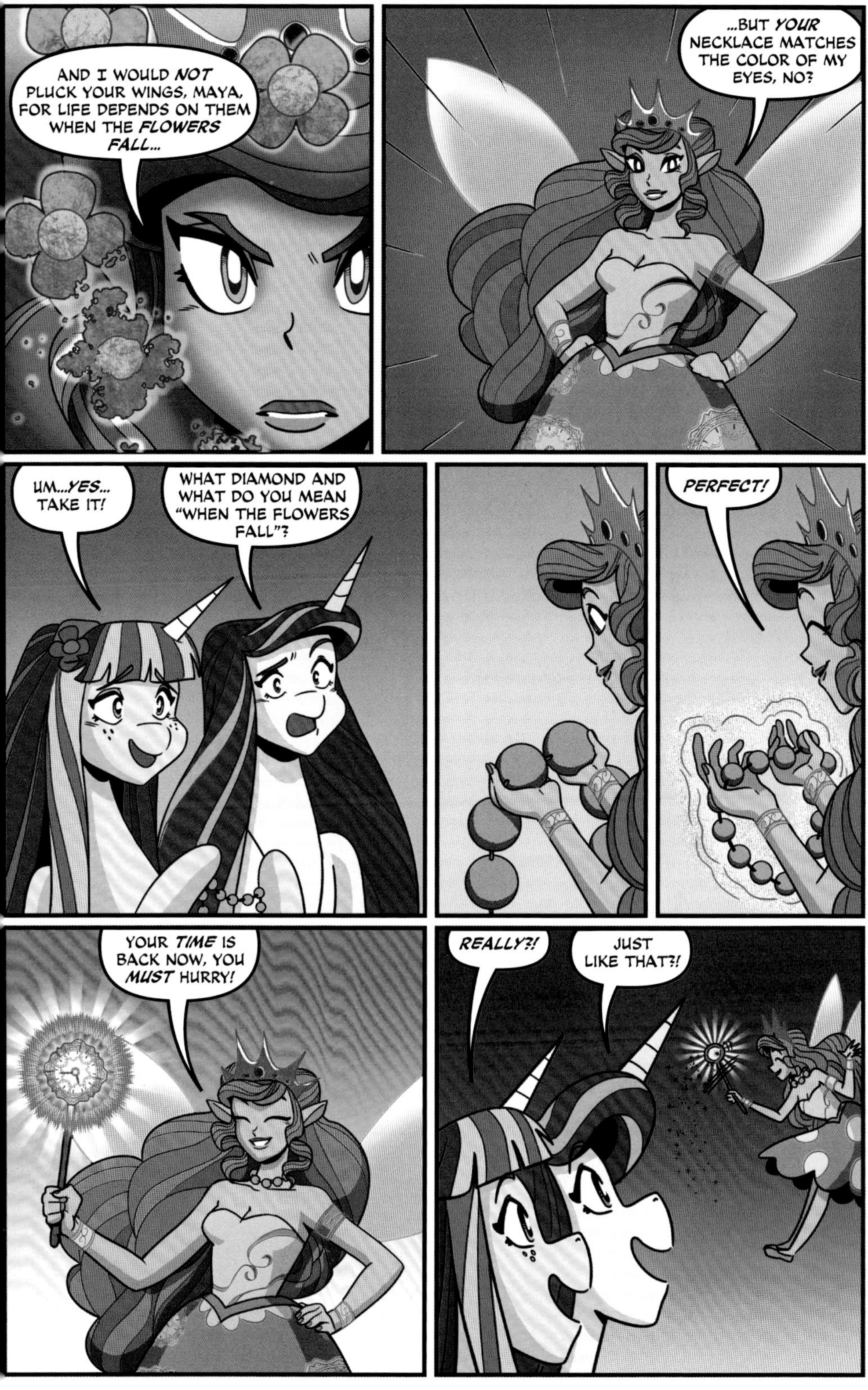
AND I WOULD *NOT* PLUCK YOUR WINGS, MAYA, FOR LIFE DEPENDS ON THEM WHEN THE *FLOWERS FALL*...
...BUT *YOUR* NECKLACE MATCHES THE COLOR OF MY EYES, NO?
UM...*YES*... TAKE IT!
WHAT DIAMOND AND WHAT DO YOU MEAN "WHEN THE FLOWERS FALL"?
PERFECT!
YOUR *TIME* IS BACK NOW, YOU *MUST* HURRY!
REALLY?!
JUST LIKE THAT?!

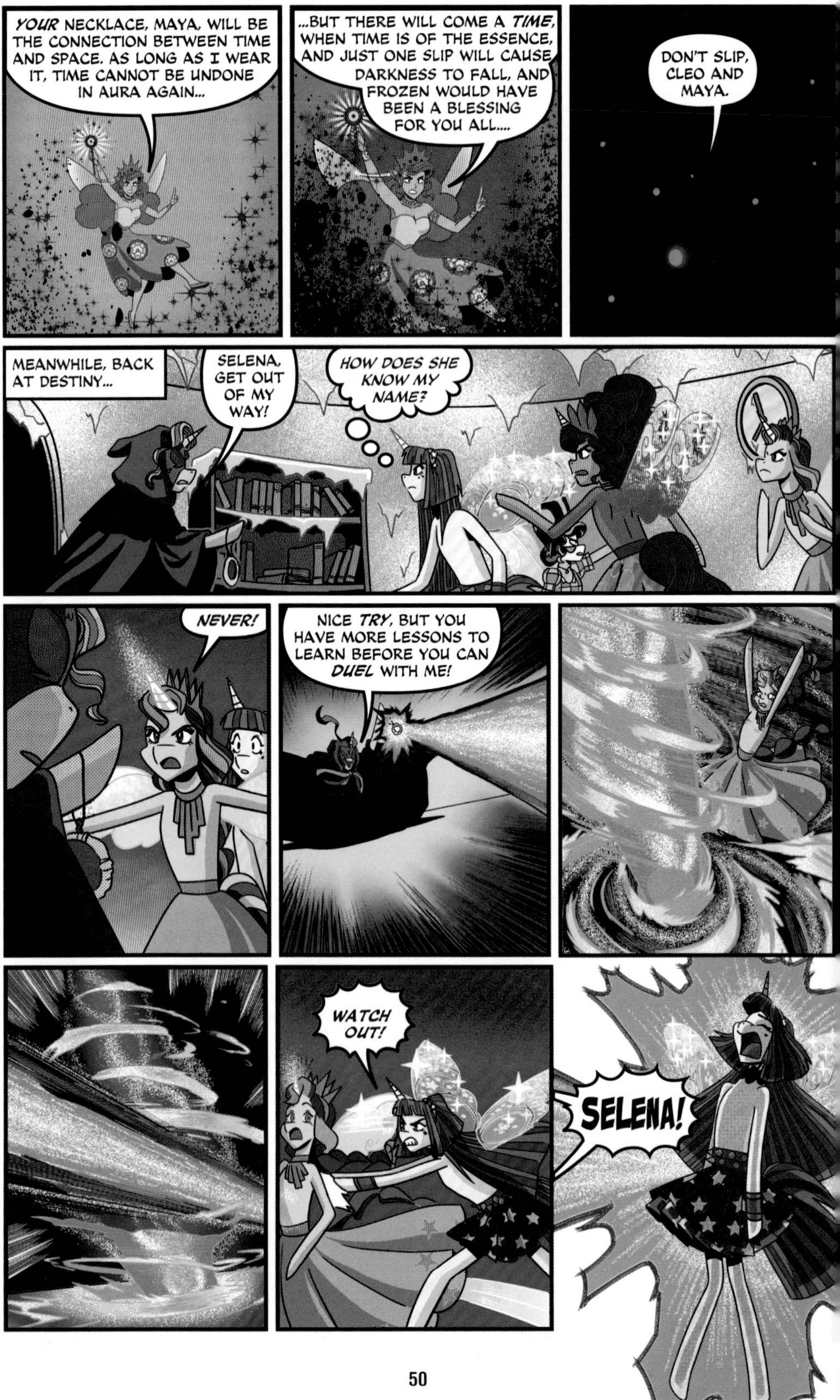
YOUR NECKLACE, MAYA, WILL BE THE CONNECTION BETWEEN TIME AND SPACE. AS LONG AS I WEAR IT, TIME CANNOT BE UNDONE IN AURA AGAIN...
...BUT THERE WILL COME A TIME, WHEN TIME IS OF THE ESSENCE, AND JUST ONE SLIP WILL CAUSE DARKNESS TO FALL, AND FROZEN WOULD HAVE BEEN A BLESSING FOR YOU ALL....
DON'T SLIP, CLEO AND MAYA.
MEANWHILE, BACK AT DESTINY...
SELENA, GET OUT OF MY WAY!
HOW DOES SHE KNOW MY NAME?
NEVER!
NICE TRY, BUT YOU HAVE MORE LESSONS TO LEARN BEFORE YOU CAN DUEL WITH ME!
WATCH OUT!
SELENA!

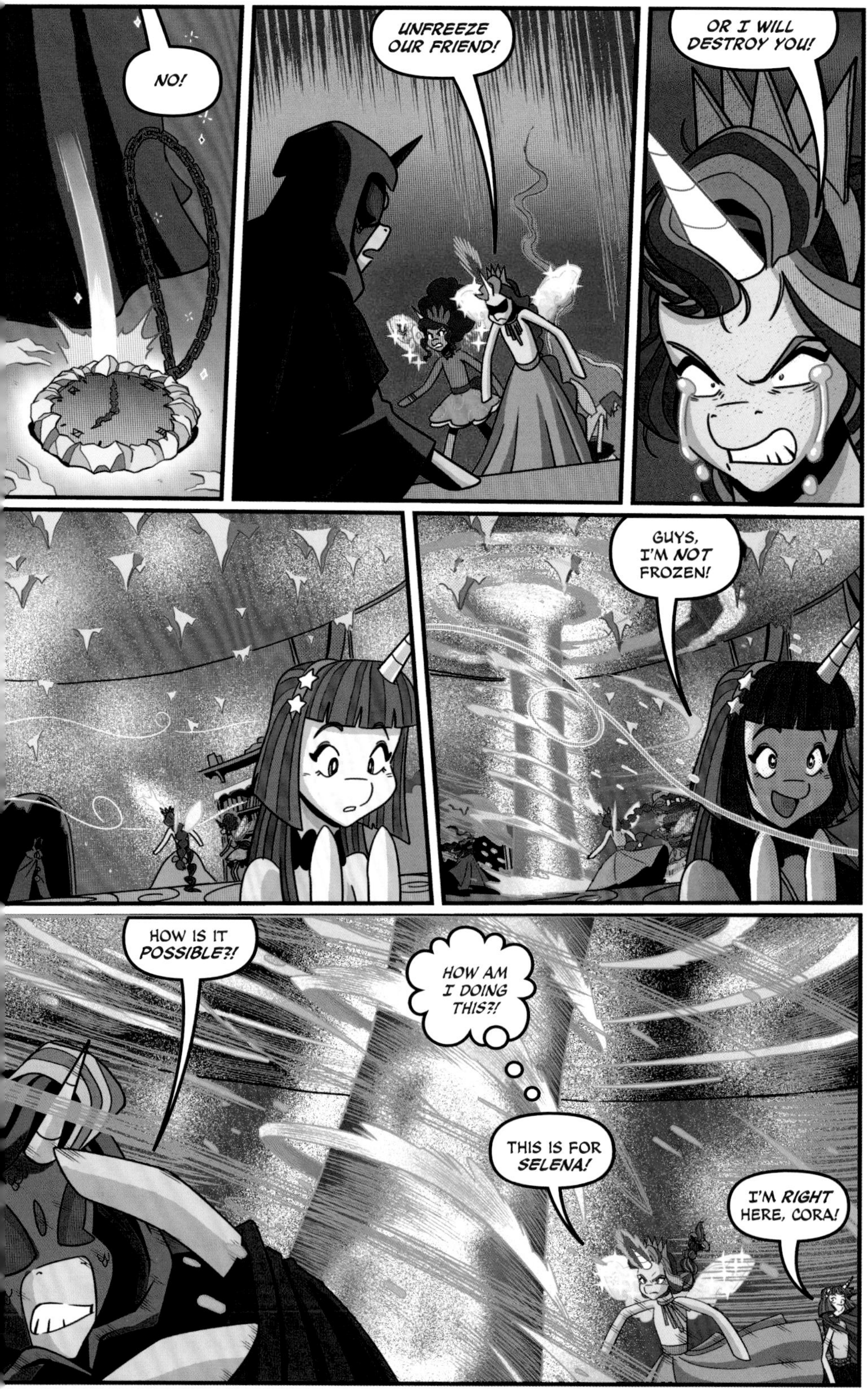
NO!
UNFREEZE OUR FRIEND!
OR I WILL DESTROY YOU!
GUYS, I'M NOT FROZEN!
HOW IS IT POSSIBLE?!
HOW AM I DOING THIS?!
THIS IS FOR SELENA!
I'M RIGHT HERE, CORA!

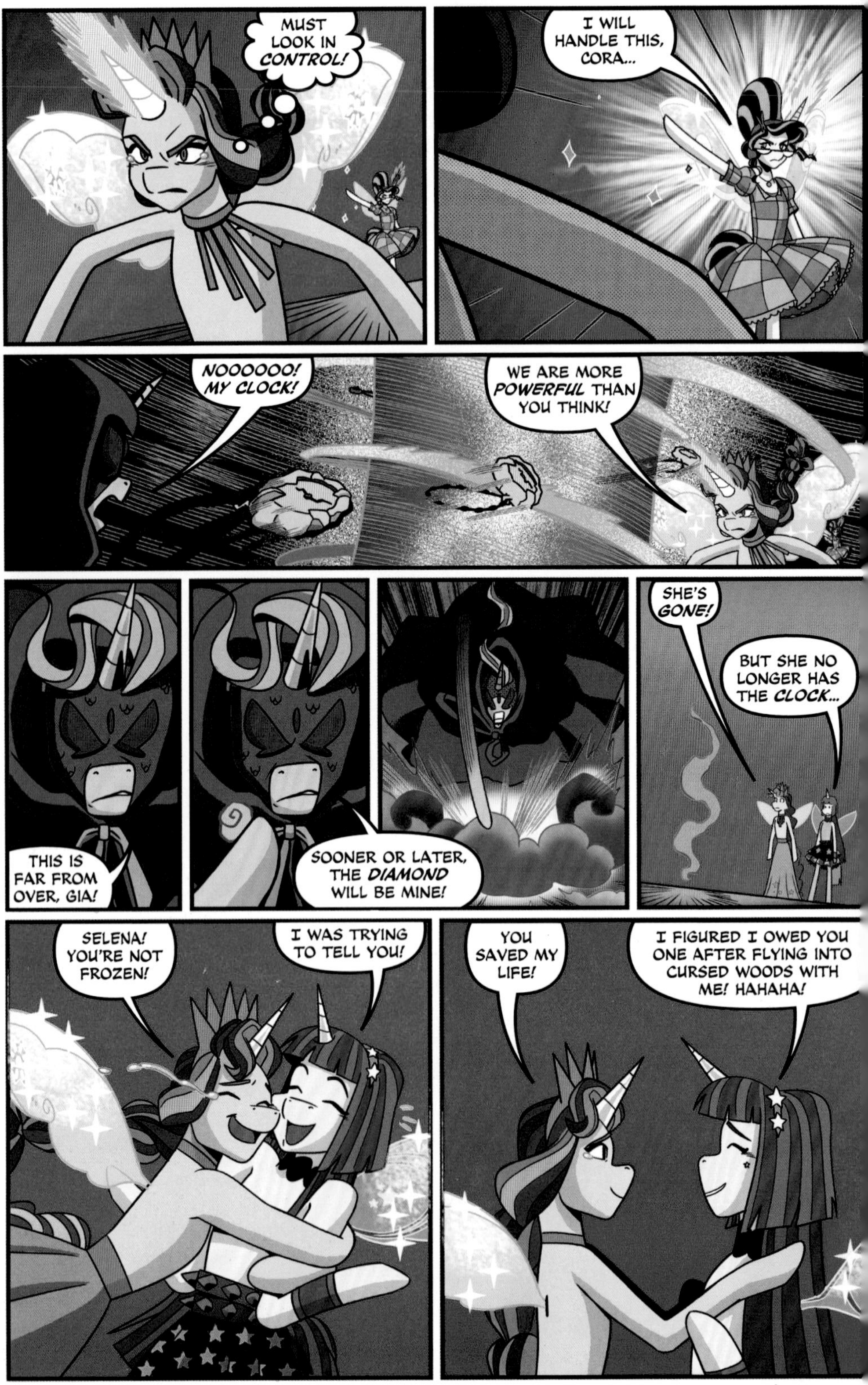
MUST LOOK IN CONTROL!
I WILL HANDLE THIS, CORA...
NOOOOOO! MY CLOCK!
WE ARE MORE POWERFUL THAN YOU THINK!
THIS IS FAR FROM OVER, GIA!
SOONER OR LATER, THE DIAMOND WILL BE MINE!
SHE'S GONE!
BUT SHE NO LONGER HAS THE CLOCK...
SELENA! YOU'RE NOT FROZEN!
I WAS TRYING TO TELL YOU!
YOU SAVED MY LIFE!
I FIGURED I OWED YOU ONE AFTER FLYING INTO CURSED WOODS WITH ME! HAHAHA!

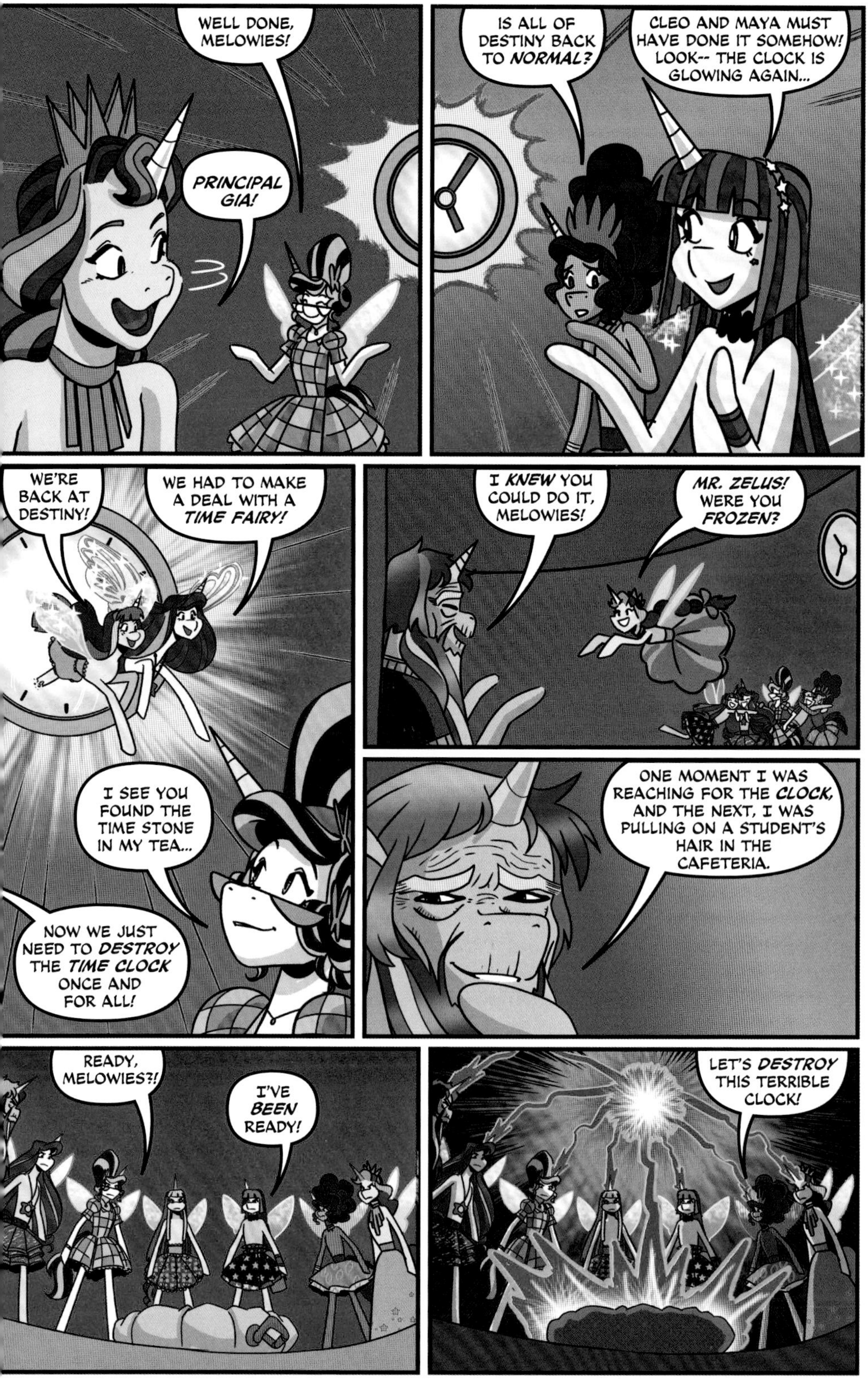
WELL DONE, MELOWIES!
PRINCIPAL GIA!
IS ALL OF DESTINY BACK TO *NORMAL?*
CLEO AND MAYA MUST HAVE DONE IT SOMEHOW! LOOK-- THE CLOCK IS GLOWING AGAIN...
WE'RE BACK AT DESTINY!
WE HAD TO MAKE A DEAL WITH A *TIME FAIRY!*
I SEE YOU FOUND THE TIME STONE IN MY TEA...
NOW WE JUST NEED TO *DESTROY* THE *TIME CLOCK* ONCE AND FOR ALL!
I *KNEW* YOU COULD DO IT, MELOWIES!
MR. ZELUS! WERE YOU *FROZEN?*
ONE MOMENT I WAS REACHING FOR THE *CLOCK,* AND THE NEXT, I WAS PULLING ON A STUDENT'S HAIR IN THE CAFETERIA.
READY, MELOWIES?!
I'VE *BEEN* READY!
LET'S *DESTROY* THIS TERRIBLE CLOCK!

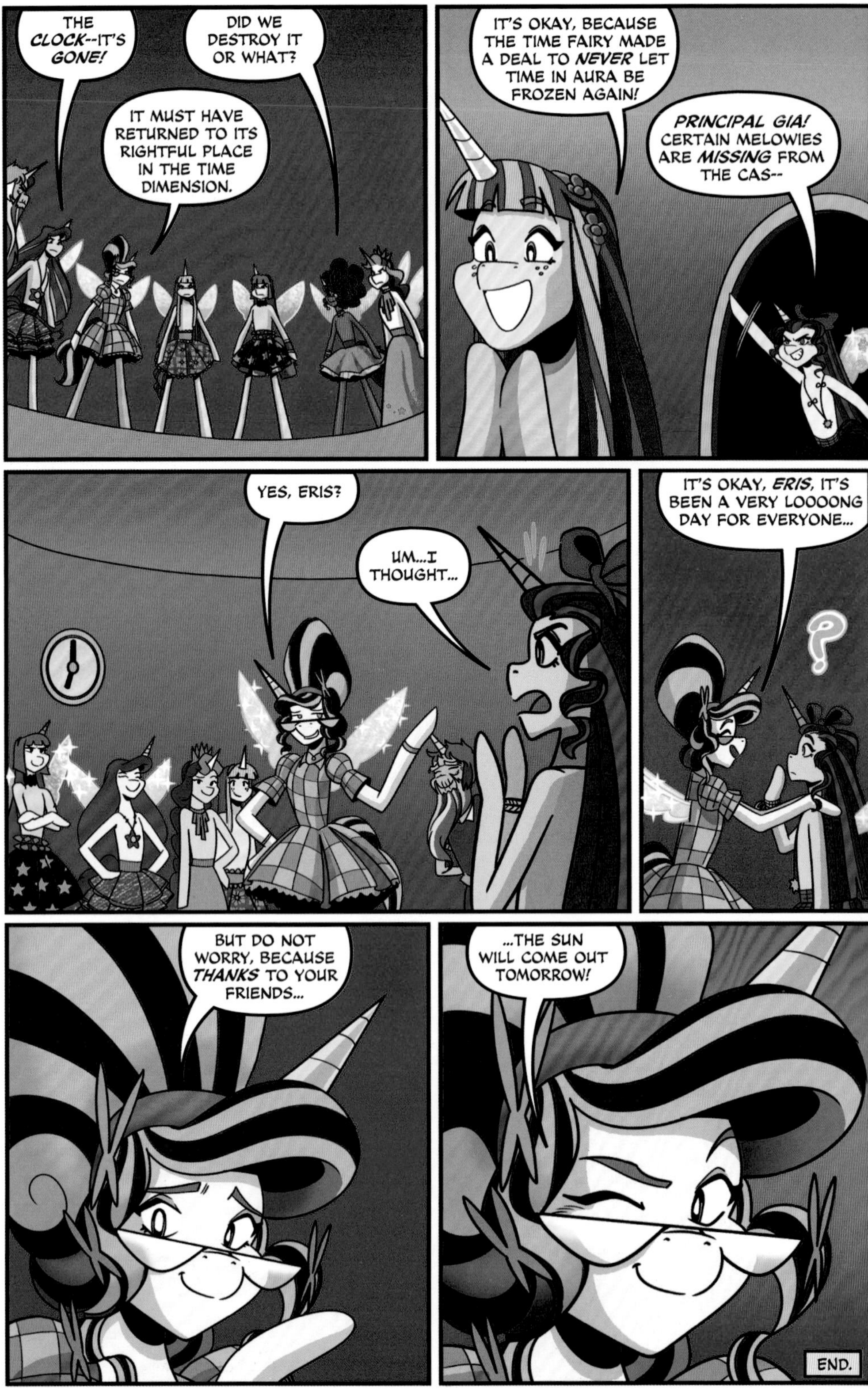
THE CLOCK--IT'S GONE!
DID WE DESTROY IT OR WHAT?
IT MUST HAVE RETURNED TO ITS RIGHTFUL PLACE IN THE TIME DIMENSION.
IT'S OKAY, BECAUSE THE TIME FAIRY MADE A DEAL TO NEVER LET TIME IN AURA BE FROZEN AGAIN!
PRINCIPAL GIA! CERTAIN MELOWIES ARE MISSING FROM THE CAS--
YES, ERIS?
UM...I THOUGHT...
IT'S OKAY, ERIS, IT'S BEEN A VERY LOOOONG DAY FOR EVERYONE...
BUT DO NOT WORRY, BECAUSE THANKS TO YOUR FRIENDS...
...THE SUN WILL COME OUT TOMORROW!
END.

WATCH OUT FOR PAPERCUTZ™

Welcome to the fantasy-filled fourth MELOWY graphic novel, by Cortney Powell, writer, and Ryan Jampole, artist, based on the characters created by Danielle Star, brought to you by Papercutz, those magical true believers dedicated to publishing great graphic novels for all ages. I'm Jim Salicrup, the Editor-in-Chief and unofficial Destiny Timekeeper, here to offer a behind-the-scenes peek at the creators who produce MELOWY. In MELOWY #2 "The Fashion Club of Colors," we offered short biographies of MELOWY creator, Danielle Star, graphic novel writer, Cortney Powell, and graphic novel artist Ryan Jampole. While writers and artists are incredibly important to any graphic novel, also important are the artists who add the lettering (the word balloons, captions, sound effects, etc.) and the color. On MELOWY, we're fortunate to have a letterer and colorist who are amongst the very best in comics. Let's meet them now...

Laurie E. Smith has been a professional comicbook colorist for the last 25 years. She lives in Winnipeg with her husband, fellow artist George Freeman. Laurie earned a B.A. (Honors) in English from the University of Winnipeg and has taught courses on comic art at various technical colleges in her home province. In 1996 she was nominated for an Eisner Award for her work on "*The X-Files*" series of comics. Although art is her profession, writing has been a lifelong love and she recently published her first science fiction novel, "The Codex of Desire," under the pen name Lauren Alder.

Laurie is incredibly talented — just look at how beautiful the color is in every MELOWY graphic novel — yet she's very modest. She's also a true professional in every sense — always doing a great job and meeting her deadlines.

We'd also like to thank the multi-talented **JayJay Jackson**, who stepped in at the last minute, when Laurie had to bow out, to complete the coloring for this volume's MELOWY story. As usual, she did an exceptional job. JayJay is an author, artist, and so many other things that if we listed them all, we'd have no room left to run Wilson Ramos Jr.'s mini-bio. Longtime Papercutz fans may even recall that JayJay wrote, drew, lettered, colored, and just about everything else on the CARDOLL "Secrets & Dreams" graphic novel we published back in 2013. JayJay continues to contribute to Papercutz in many ways and we can't possibly thank her enough.

Wilson Ramos Jr. is a freelance comic artist who has worked in the comic industry for over 25 years. He has worked as a colorist, letterer, inker, penciller, and art director in digital and print comics, posters, brochures, trading cards, magazines and scores of projects for Marvel Comics, DC Comics, Dark Horse, Random House, Papercutz, and many others. His recent projects include the Independent Publisher Book Award-winning *God Woke* written by the legendary Stan Lee. Wilson is also a popular sketch card artist who has work for Topps, Upper Deck, Cryptozoic Entertainment, and Dynamite Entertainment. In his spare time, Wilson works on his creator-owned comicbooks *Team Kaiju* and *Ninja Mouse* published by Section 8 Comics.

Ramos lives in New York City, where he attended The High School of Art & Design. He received his Bachelor's of Fine Arts Degree in Graphic Design from Mercy College. Wilson has been working full-time as a freelance artist, after working on staff for several years at Marvel Comics.

Like Laurie, Wilson is super-talented, modest, and a true pro. We're very happy to have such top talents contribute not only to MELOWY, but to other Papercutz graphic novels as well. For example, both Laurie and Wilson also color and letter another Papercutz series, drawn by Ryan Jampole, about five fabulous females who attend a special school together. No, we're not talking about THEA STILTON (although they did work on that series too!), but a series written by a 12 year-old girl and her mom. It's called GEEKY F@B 5, and it's by Lucy and Liz Lareau, writers, along with Ryan, Laurie, and Wilson. Basically, it's more of an earth-bound version of MELOWY, with the magic coming from what can happen when girls stick together. But for an even better idea of what GEEK F@B 5 is about, check out the preview of GEEKY F@B 5 #1 "It's Not Rocket Science" on the following pages.*

Of course, all you favorite flying fillies will return in MELOWY #5 "Melloween," coming to your favorite bookseller or library soon. It's not like they're frozen in time or something!

Thanks,

Jim

*For the record, Laurie E. Smith didn't color GEEKY F@B 5 #1–Matt Herms did — but she has colored pages in the following volumes of GF5!

STAY IN TOUCH!

EMAIL: salicrup@papercutz.com
WEB: papercutz.com
TWITTER: @papercutzgn
INSTAGRAM: @papercutzgn
FACEBOOK: PAPERCUTZGRAPHICNOVELS
FANMAIL: Papercutz, 160 Broadway, Suite 700, East Wing, New York, NY 10038

Here's a special preview of GEEKY F@B 5
"It's Not Rocket Science"

Chapter One: First Day. New School.

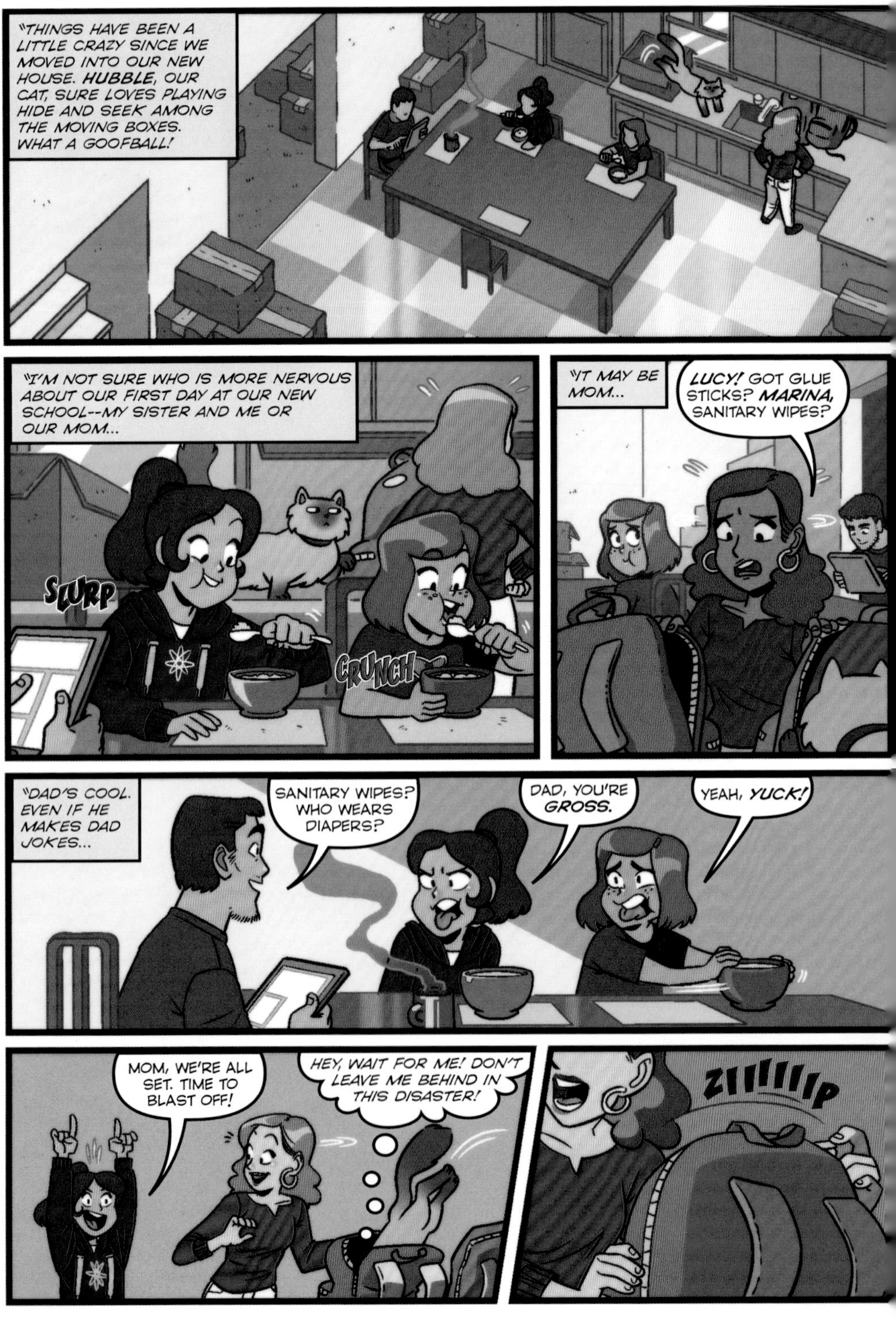

"THINGS HAVE BEEN A LITTLE CRAZY SINCE WE MOVED INTO OUR NEW HOUSE. HUBBLE, OUR CAT, SURE LOVES PLAYING HIDE AND SEEK AMONG THE MOVING BOXES. WHAT A GOOFBALL!
"I'M NOT SURE WHO IS MORE NERVOUS ABOUT OUR FIRST DAY AT OUR NEW SCHOOL--MY SISTER AND ME OR OUR MOM...
SLURP
CRUNCH
"IT MAY BE MOM...
LUCY! GOT GLUE STICKS? MARINA, SANITARY WIPES?
"DAD'S COOL. EVEN IF HE MAKES DAD JOKES...
SANITARY WIPES? WHO WEARS DIAPERS?
DAD, YOU'RE GROSS.
YEAH, YUCK!
MOM, WE'RE ALL SET. TIME TO BLAST OFF!
HEY, WAIT FOR ME! DON'T LEAVE ME BEHIND IN THIS DISASTER!
ZIIIIIIP

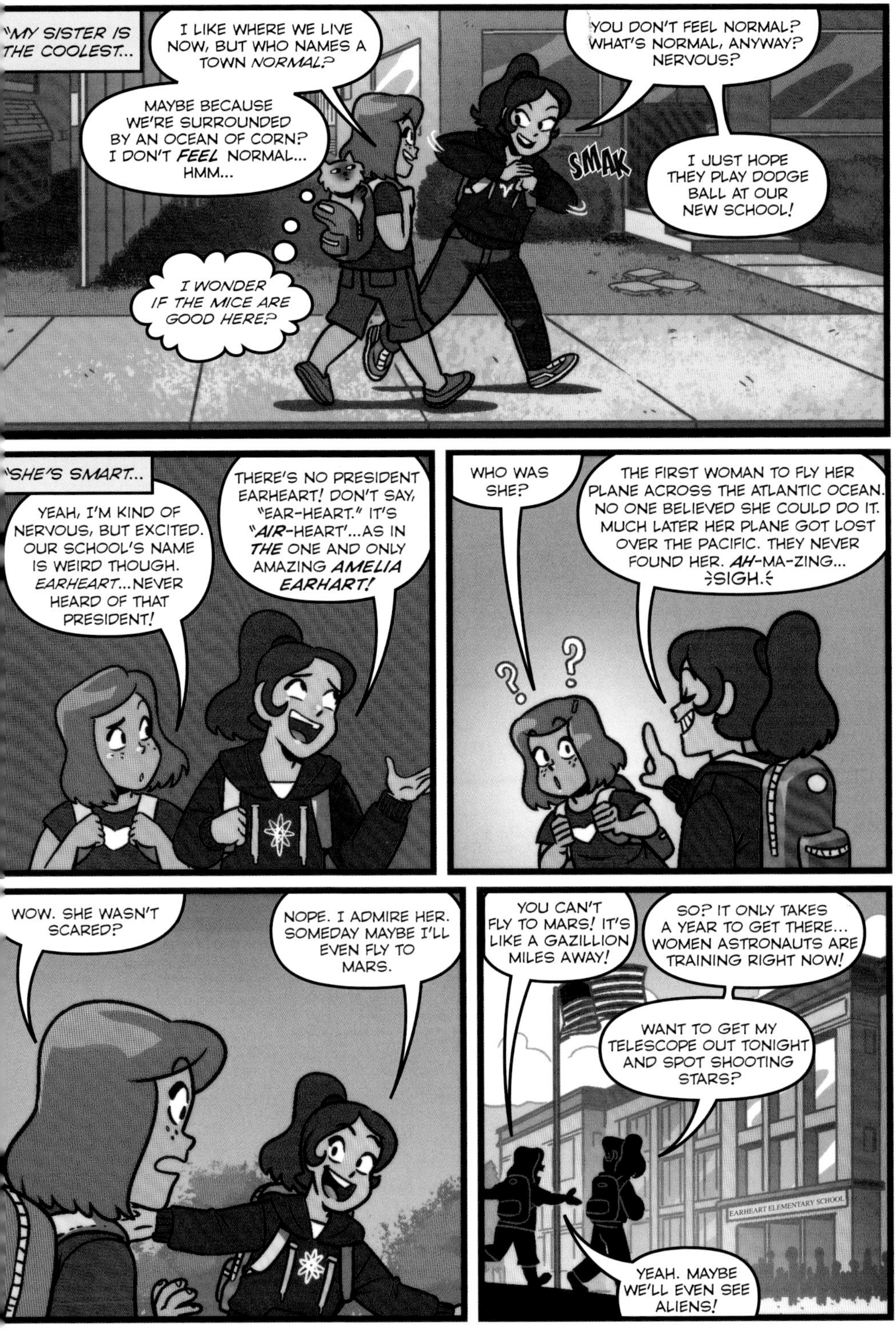
"MY SISTER IS THE COOLEST...
I LIKE WHERE WE LIVE NOW, BUT WHO NAMES A TOWN NORMAL?
MAYBE BECAUSE WE'RE SURROUNDED BY AN OCEAN OF CORN? I DON'T FEEL NORMAL... HMM...
I WONDER IF THE MICE ARE GOOD HERE?
YOU DON'T FEEL NORMAL? WHAT'S NORMAL, ANYWAY? NERVOUS?
SMAK
I JUST HOPE THEY PLAY DODGE BALL AT OUR NEW SCHOOL!
"SHE'S SMART...
YEAH, I'M KIND OF NERVOUS, BUT EXCITED. OUR SCHOOL'S NAME IS WEIRD THOUGH. EARHEART...NEVER HEARD OF THAT PRESIDENT!
THERE'S NO PRESIDENT EARHEART! DON'T SAY, "EAR-HEART." IT'S "AIR-HEART"...AS IN THE ONE AND ONLY AMAZING AMELIA EARHART!
WHO WAS SHE?
THE FIRST WOMAN TO FLY HER PLANE ACROSS THE ATLANTIC OCEAN. NO ONE BELIEVED SHE COULD DO IT. MUCH LATER HER PLANE GOT LOST OVER THE PACIFIC. THEY NEVER FOUND HER. AH-MA-ZING... SIGH.
WOW. SHE WASN'T SCARED?
NOPE. I ADMIRE HER. SOMEDAY MAYBE I'LL EVEN FLY TO MARS.
YOU CAN'T FLY TO MARS! IT'S LIKE A GAZILLION MILES AWAY!
SO? IT ONLY TAKES A YEAR TO GET THERE... WOMEN ASTRONAUTS ARE TRAINING RIGHT NOW!
WANT TO GET MY TELESCOPE OUT TONIGHT AND SPOT SHOOTING STARS?
EARHEART ELEMENTARY SCHOOL
YEAH. MAYBE WE'LL EVEN SEE ALIENS!

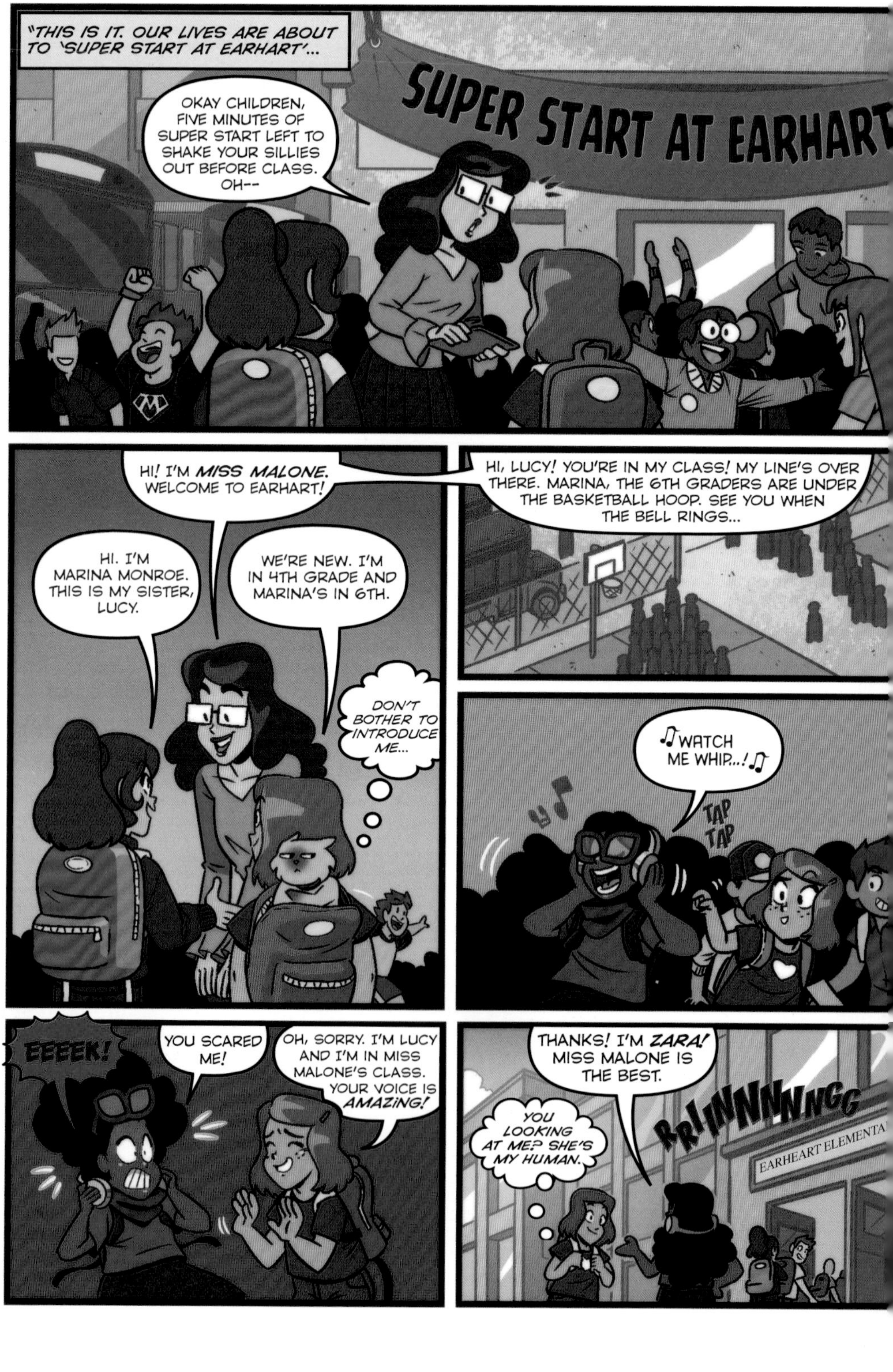
"THIS IS IT. OUR LIVES ARE ABOUT TO 'SUPER START AT EARHART'...
SUPER START AT EARHART
OKAY CHILDREN, FIVE MINUTES OF SUPER START LEFT TO SHAKE YOUR SILLIES OUT BEFORE CLASS. OH--
HI! I'M MISS MALONE. WELCOME TO EARHART!
HI. I'M MARINA MONROE. THIS IS MY SISTER, LUCY.
WE'RE NEW. I'M IN 4TH GRADE AND MARINA'S IN 6TH.
DON'T BOTHER TO INTRODUCE ME...
HI, LUCY! YOU'RE IN MY CLASS! MY LINE'S OVER THERE. MARINA, THE 6TH GRADERS ARE UNDER THE BASKETBALL HOOP. SEE YOU WHEN THE BELL RINGS...
♫WATCH ME WHIP...!♫
TAP TAP
EEEEK!
YOU SCARED ME!
OH, SORRY. I'M LUCY AND I'M IN MISS MALONE'S CLASS. YOUR VOICE IS AMAZING!
THANKS! I'M ZARA! MISS MALONE IS THE BEST.
RRIINNNNNNGG
YOU LOOKING AT ME? SHE'S MY HUMAN.
EARHEART ELEMENTA

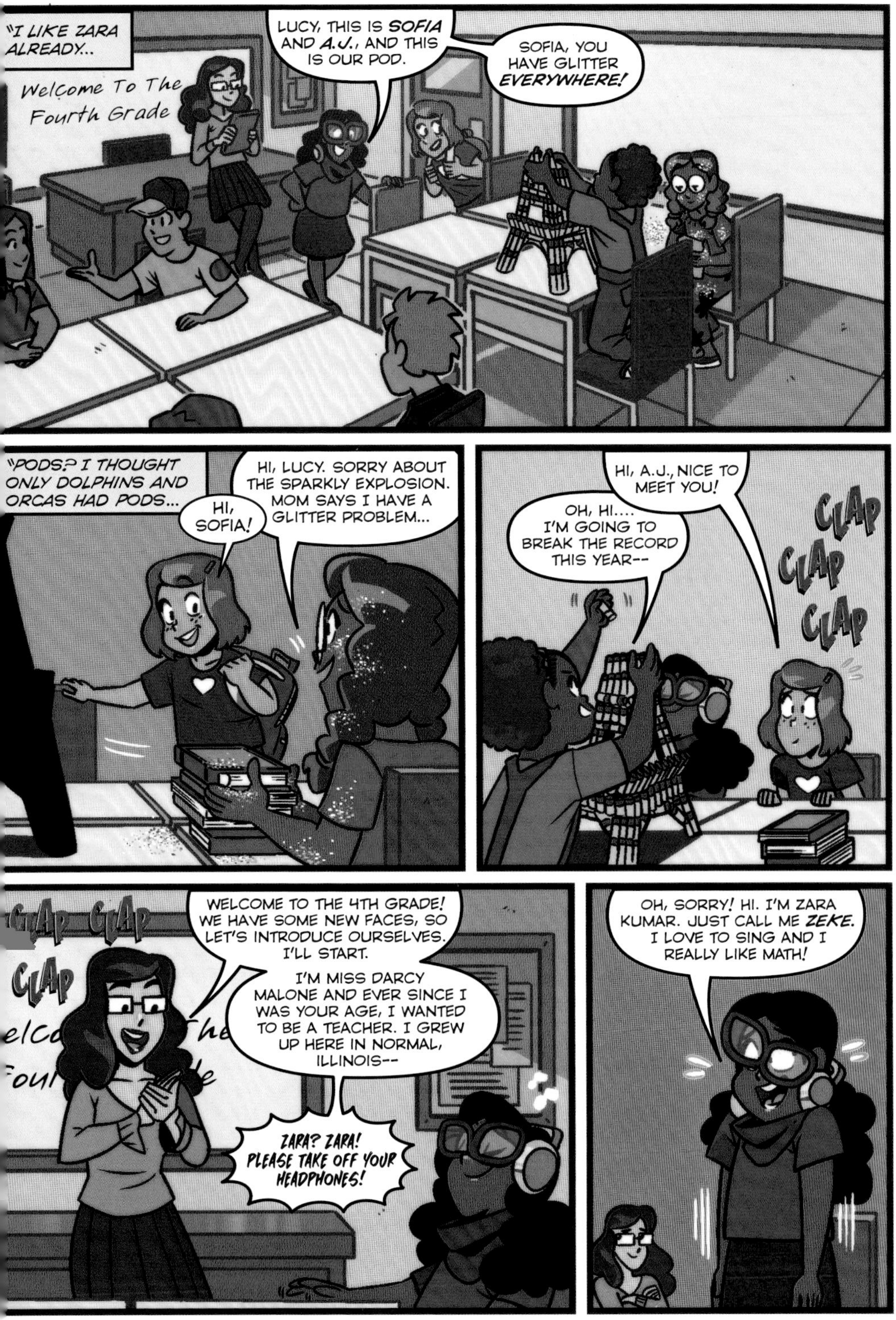
"I LIKE ZARA ALREADY...
Welcome To The Fourth Grade
LUCY, THIS IS SOFIA AND A.J., AND THIS IS OUR POD.
SOFIA, YOU HAVE GLITTER EVERYWHERE!
"PODS? I THOUGHT ONLY DOLPHINS AND ORCAS HAD PODS...
HI, SOFIA!
HI, LUCY. SORRY ABOUT THE SPARKLY EXPLOSION. MOM SAYS I HAVE A GLITTER PROBLEM...
HI, A.J., NICE TO MEET YOU!
OH, HI.... I'M GOING TO BREAK THE RECORD THIS YEAR--
CLAP
CLAP
CLAP
CLAP CLAP
CLAP
WELCOME TO THE 4TH GRADE! WE HAVE SOME NEW FACES, SO LET'S INTRODUCE OURSELVES. I'LL START.
I'M MISS DARCY MALONE AND EVER SINCE I WAS YOUR AGE, I WANTED TO BE A TEACHER. I GREW UP HERE IN NORMAL, ILLINOIS--
ZARA? ZARA! PLEASE TAKE OFF YOUR HEADPHONES!
OH, SORRY! HI. I'M ZARA KUMAR. JUST CALL ME ZEKE. I LOVE TO SING AND I REALLY LIKE MATH!

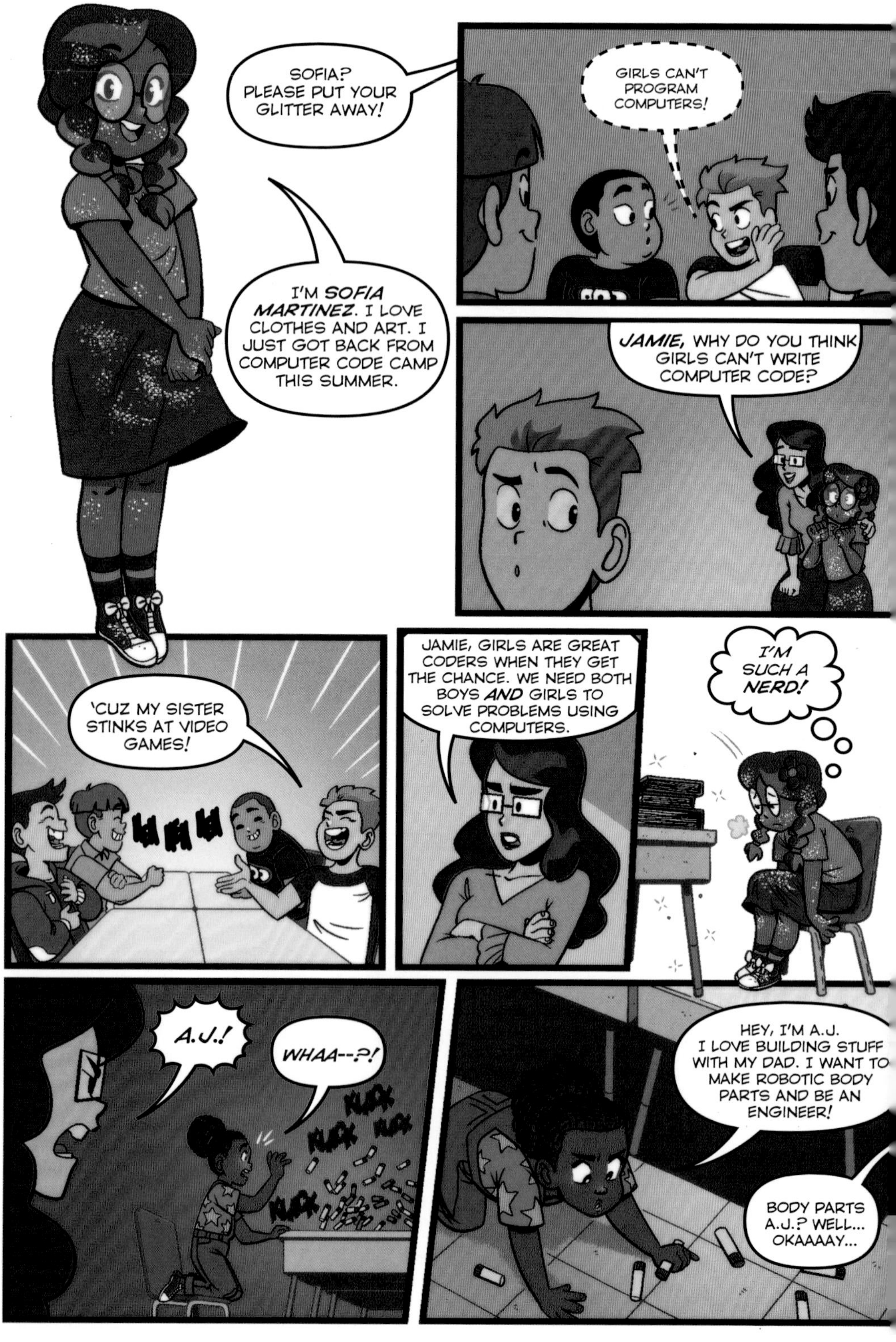

I'M SOFIA MARTINEZ. I LOVE CLOTHES AND ART. I JUST GOT BACK FROM COMPUTER CODE CAMP THIS SUMMER.
SOFIA? PLEASE PUT YOUR GLITTER AWAY!
GIRLS CAN'T PROGRAM COMPUTERS!
JAMIE, WHY DO YOU THINK GIRLS CAN'T WRITE COMPUTER CODE?
'CUZ MY SISTER STINKS AT VIDEO GAMES!
JAMIE, GIRLS ARE GREAT CODERS WHEN THEY GET THE CHANCE. WE NEED BOTH BOYS AND GIRLS TO SOLVE PROBLEMS USING COMPUTERS.
I'M SUCH A NERD!
A.J.!
WHAA--?!
HEY, I'M A.J. I LOVE BUILDING STUFF WITH MY DAD. I WANT TO MAKE ROBOTIC BODY PARTS AND BE AN ENGINEER!
BODY PARTS A.J.? WELL... OKAAAAY...

HOW ABOUT YOU, LUCY?

HI, MY NAME IS *LUCY MONROE*. I JUST MOVED HERE FROM VIRGINIA. I LOVE ANIMALS AND TREES BUT...

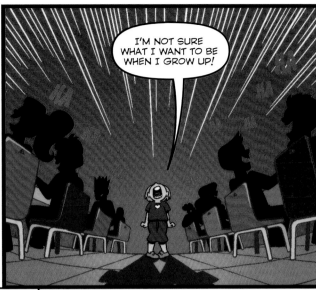

I'M NOT SURE WHAT I WANT TO BE WHEN I GROW UP!

THAT'S ENOUGH, CLASS! DON'T WORRY, LUCY. YOU'VE GOT TIME.

THAT'S WHAT SCHOOL IS ALL ABOUT!

"THAT'S JUST GREAT, I'VE MADE A FOOL OF MYSELF ON THE FIRST DAY...

EVERYONE, READY TO START FOURTH GRADE?

YEAH! GIMME SOME FRACTIONS!

THAT'S WHEN I FINALLY NOTICED...

HUBBLE! WHAT ARE YOU DOING? YOU ARE SO STUCK THERE FOR THE DAY.

NOT A MEOW OUT OF YOU, MISTER!

FINE, I'LL TAKE A NAP THEN. WAKE ME FOR LUNCH. I LOVE ME SOME TATER TOTS.

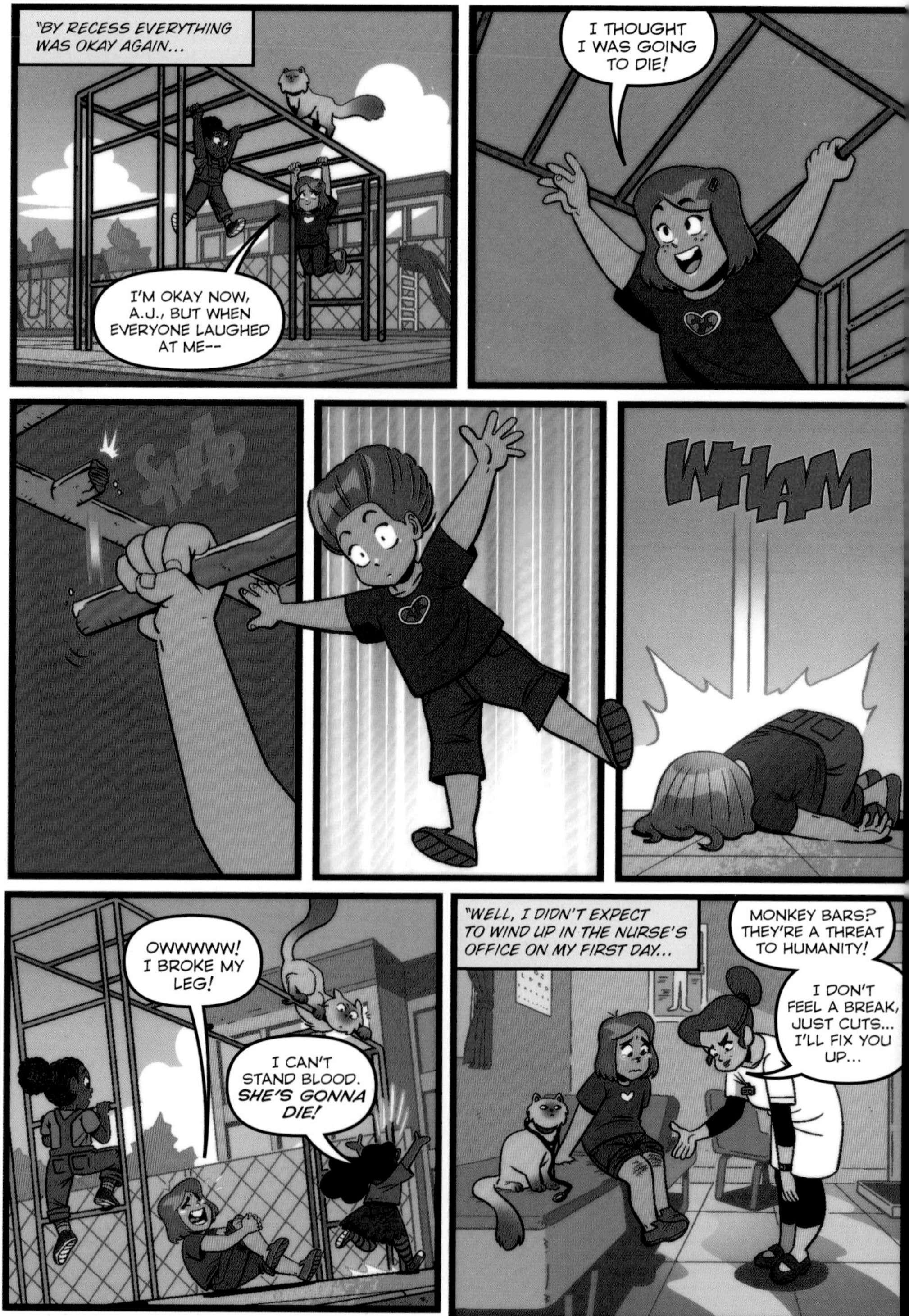
"BY RECESS EVERYTHING WAS OKAY AGAIN...
I'M OKAY NOW, A.J., BUT WHEN EVERYONE LAUGHED AT ME--
I THOUGHT I WAS GOING TO DIE!
WHAM
OWWWWW! I BROKE MY LEG!
I CAN'T STAND BLOOD. SHE'S GONNA DIE!
"WELL, I DIDN'T EXPECT TO WIND UP IN THE NURSE'S OFFICE ON MY FIRST DAY...
MONKEY BARS? THEY'RE A THREAT TO HUMANITY!
I DON'T FEEL A BREAK, JUST CUTS... I'LL FIX YOU UP...

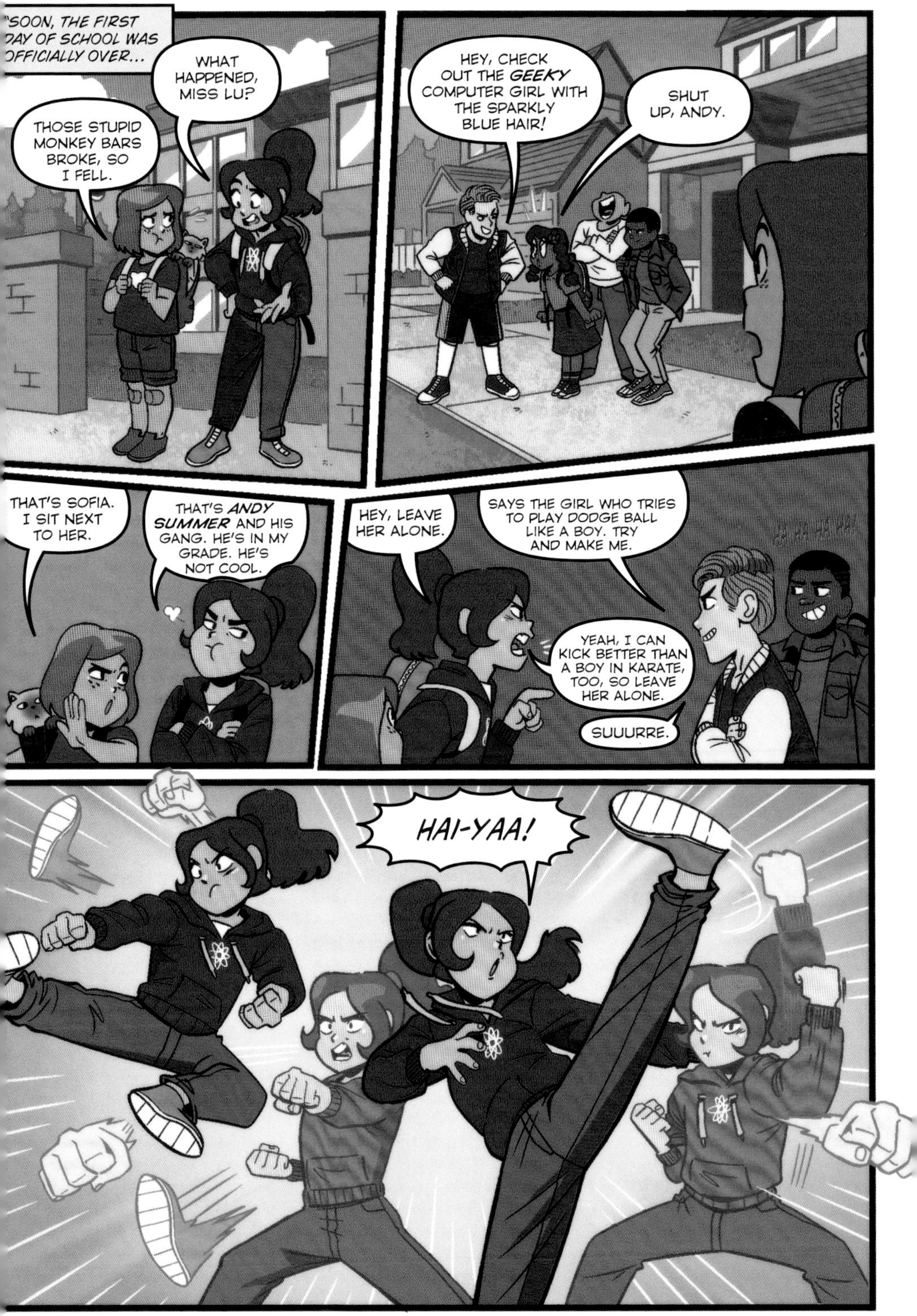
SOON, THE FIRST DAY OF SCHOOL WAS OFFICIALLY OVER...
WHAT HAPPENED, MISS LU?
THOSE STUPID MONKEY BARS BROKE, SO I FELL.
HEY, CHECK OUT THE GEEKY COMPUTER GIRL WITH THE SPARKLY BLUE HAIR!
SHUT UP, ANDY.
THAT'S SOFIA. I SIT NEXT TO HER.
THAT'S ANDY SUMMER AND HIS GANG. HE'S IN MY GRADE. HE'S NOT COOL.
HEY, LEAVE HER ALONE.
SAYS THE GIRL WHO TRIES TO PLAY DODGE BALL LIKE A BOY. TRY AND MAKE ME.
YEAH, I CAN KICK BETTER THAN A BOY IN KARATE, TOO, SO LEAVE HER ALONE.
SUUURRE.
HAI-YAA!

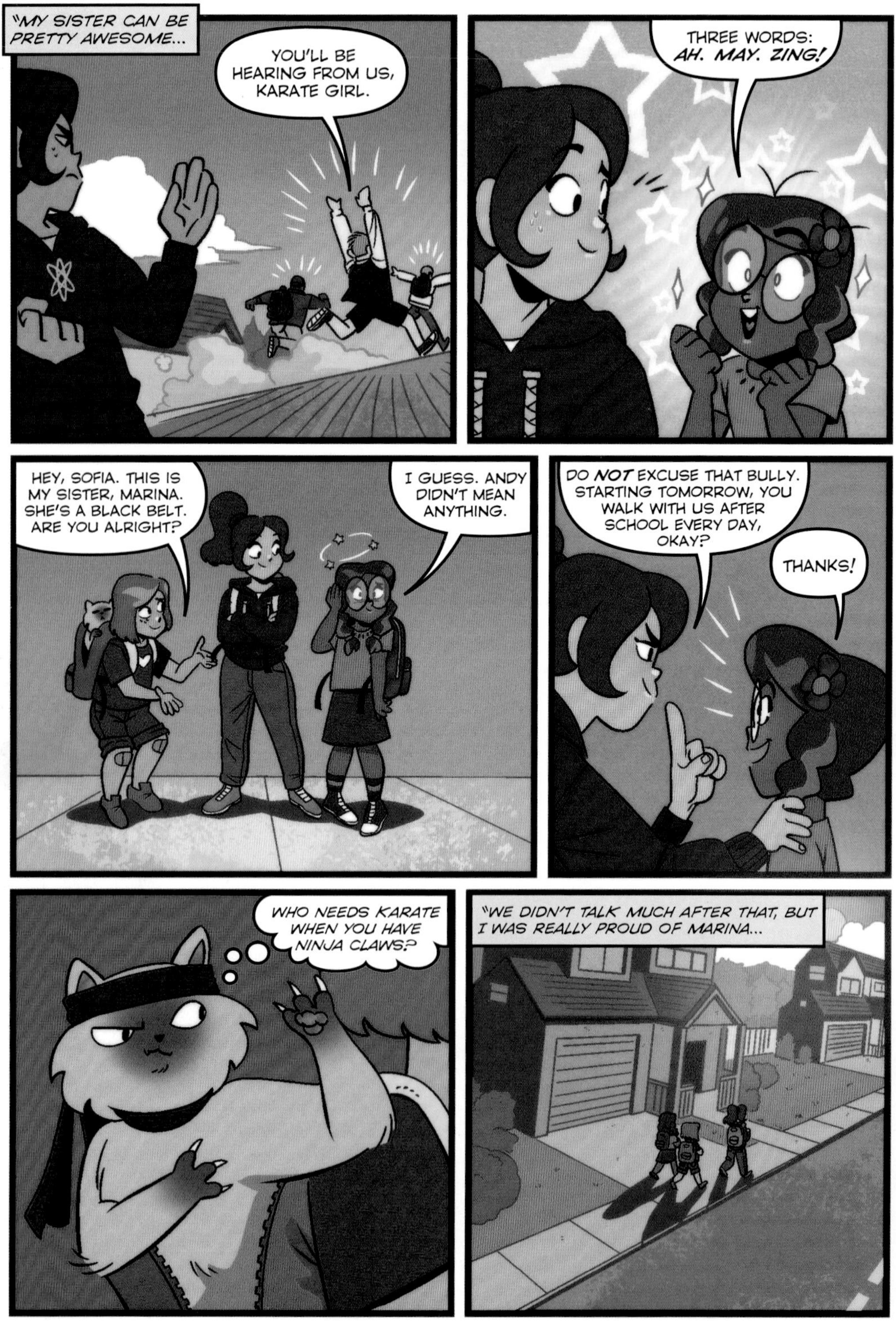
"MY SISTER CAN BE PRETTY AWESOME...
YOU'LL BE HEARING FROM US, KARATE GIRL.
THREE WORDS: AH. MAY. ZING!
HEY, SOFIA. THIS IS MY SISTER, MARINA. SHE'S A BLACK BELT. ARE YOU ALRIGHT?
I GUESS. ANDY DIDN'T MEAN ANYTHING.
DO NOT EXCUSE THAT BULLY. STARTING TOMORROW, YOU WALK WITH US AFTER SCHOOL EVERY DAY, OKAY?
THANKS!
WHO NEEDS KARATE WHEN YOU HAVE NINJA CLAWS?
"WE DIDN'T TALK MUCH AFTER THAT, BUT I WAS REALLY PROUD OF MARINA...

Don't miss GEEKY F@B 5 #1 "It's Not Rocket Science" available at booksellers and libraries now.